Espíritu

by B. K. Miller

PRESS

To all those who encouraged me and inspired
me along the way,
to my parents who gave me my faith and my love
for books,
to my sister Trevi who consistently supported me
and put up with me throughout the duration
of this project,
to Brandon and Michael—two noble warriors,
to the amazing women who have served as spiritual
mentors in my life,
to the fourth graders of Lucas, Texas,
to the Jones family whose house on the farm
provided me with countless magical childhood
memories and much of the inspiration
for this book…

and to the late Bob Dellinger—who believed in
my dream.

I finally fell asleep—my head resting on the pages of light. I dreamed of battles and sword fights and knights fighting dragons. In one of my dreams, I was one of the knights. The dragon had no power over me because I was fighting with the sword of Espíritu—the most powerful sword in the world.

Spencer,

Merry Christmas!! May your life be a great adventure in Christ!

A.B.K. Miller

Ephesians 6:12

Pronunciation Guide

Espíritu = eh-SPEE-ree-too

Paraíso = pah-RYE-soh

criado = cree-AH-doh

Mensajero = men-sah-HEH-roh

Fuego = FWEH-goh

Risa = REE-sah

Dulce = DOOL-seh

Nieve-nube = Nee-EH-veh NOO-beh

Lamento = lah-MEN-toh

sombra = SOHM-brah

Mentiroso = men-tee-ROH-soh

Engaño = en-GAHN-yoh

Miedo = mee-EH-doh

Orgullo = or-GOO-yoh

Contents

CHAPTER 1

Sara

The last words my mother spoke to me before she died were, "I'm going away now to a better place. Take care of your Dad, will you, Sara? He will need your help."

Help? Help with what? I didn't know, but I didn't care. My mother was dying, and that's all I cared about. Where was she going? Would I ever see her again? I was only six years old—I didn't understand.

Now I was ten. I learned a lot in those four years—like never to believe someone when they say they'll always be there for you. Like the job of a father is basically to ignore his children. And like uncles who don't speak your language can be *extremely* annoying.

Well, at least uncles who don't *often* speak your language. My Uncle Antonio was born in Mexico, so that made him Mexican. I was born in America, so that made me American—not *Mexican*-American. How come every time people looked at me, they automatically assumed I spoke Spanish? Just because I had the dark skin, dark hair, and dark eyes didn't mean anything. It didn't mean that I knew how to speak some foreign language.

But my dad's brother did. Uncle Antonio grew up in Mexico, so of course *he* knew Spanish. My dad grew up in Mexico, too, but he didn't speak the language nearly as often as Uncle Antonio did. (My dad didn't speak much of *any* language—not after my mother died, anyway).

Aunt Sarah was different from both of them. She didn't speak Spanish at all because she was American (like me). She married my Uncle Antonio after he moved here from Mexico. There was always something about Aunt Sarah that bothered me; maybe it was the way she talked. She had this nicey-nice way of talking that made me just want to throw up. Maybe it was the way her long, blond hair swished when she walked. Or maybe it was the way she looked at me; every time her bright blue eyes met mine, I felt as if she were invading my privacy, somehow. Her eyes were so *bright*— almost as if a light were shining in them. Anyway, for whatever reason, I tried to avoid Aunt Sarah as much as possible.

Jaime was a disgusting combination of them both. (Mixed children are nearly always annoyingly attractive.) My seven-year-old cousin had jet-black hair and shiny blue eyes, creating a contrast that caused him to look—as my mother used to say—"stunning." The only stunning thing about him, I thought, was his ability to get on my nerves. Every time I would go over to Uncle Antonio's house to visit (which was nearly every summer of my entire life), I could count on Jaime to try and make my stay there as miserable as possible. His job, it seemed, was to follow me around everywhere with that big, annoying smile on his face *begging* me to do stuff with him. Did it never occur to him that maybe I had better things to do than to hang out with a seven-year-old?

But the worst part about having to go to Uncle Antonio's house didn't have anything (or *much*) to do with Uncle Antonio, Aunt Sarah, *or* Jaime; it had to do with my dad. If you're not an only child with only one parent, you probably won't understand. But if you are, you understand that life can get pretty lonely sometimes. Like I mentioned before, my dad didn't talk a whole lot. So that meant that I ended up spending a lot of time off by myself while my dad spent it sitting in front of the television set.

What did this have to do with going to Uncle Antonio's house? Well, for some unknown reason, my dad would open up and start talking whenever we went there—usually with Uncle Antonio. Of course, it's natural for brothers to want to talk to each other. But what I didn't understand was why my dad would talk to him and never to me.

I tried not to think about it. It does absolutely no good to worry about something that you can't change.

You may be wondering why my aunt and I have the same name (except that hers is spelled with an "h"). This may sound strange, but—since I called her "Aunt Sarah" nearly every summer of my entire life—I never even thought about it. When I *did* start thinking about it, I didn't ask. As I have mentioned previously, my dad wasn't the sort of person I could really talk to.

Maybe you can understand why—when the time came once again for our yearly summer "vacation" trip—I was less than thrilled about going. It meant time spent watching my dad ignore me (even more than usual), it meant time spent being followed around by a "stunning" seven-year-old, and it meant *lots* of time spent driving: a *nine-hour* trip by car! The sensible (and more fun) thing to do would have been to fly, but that was another thing about my dad: he didn't like to spend money on "unnecessary" things. (For some reason, anything my *dad* wanted to buy was never "unnecessary.") I'd never gotten a chance to ride in an airplane and had always wanted to. But, like usual, my dad's mind was made up.

So I prepared myself once again for a seemingly endless drive to the dullest, driest place on the face of the Earth:

southern Texas. (My dad and I lived in *eastern* Texas where there was at least vegetation—like grass and trees.) It was pretty late when we finally arrived at Uncle Antonio's house. Dad and I never left on trips until after noon because he always had to check the sports scores on TV before leaving. All that we had time to do, basically, was to say "hi" and go to bed. As soon as we arrived—and the barrage of hugs and kisses was finally over—I headed for Jaime's room where I quickly unpacked my suitcase, changed clothes, and crawled into bed. I crawled into bed for two reasons: one, because I was tired. Two, because the bed happened to be the bottom bunk of a set of bunk beds. Jaime had two much-older sisters who had left a few years earlier for college, so that left Jaime with his choice each night of either a top or a bottom bunk. (Whenever I was there, he always chose the top, which was fine with me. On the bottom bunk you don't have to worry about falling out of bed in the middle of the night and breaking your neck.)

That's always how it was. At least tomorrow I would get to see the horses.

Uncle Antonio's house was on a farm—and like on any good farm, there were horses. Of course, there were other animals, too—like chickens and roosters and cows and, one year, even turkeys. But I didn't care about any of those. All I cared about were the horses.

You see, I'd always loved horses—ever since I was little. Even though I'd never owned one (because, as Dad pointed out, they were "unnecessary"), I'd always wanted one. I would oftentimes stand on the wooden gate of the corral and imagine which one I would choose for myself—just in case Uncle Antonio ever decided to let me have one (and just in case Dad ever had a change of heart). The choice was a difficult one; there were chestnuts, bays, sorrels, pintos, blacks, and even a dappled gray one.

But not a white one. Throughout all the years I'd visited

Uncle Antonio's farm, they had never owned a single white horse. This was maddening to me. White horses were quite simply the most beautiful creatures on the face of the Earth. I loved watching them prance down the street in parades adorned with bright colors. I loved watching them leap gracefully over hurdles in horse show competitions. I loved watching them in movies with knights in shining armor on their backs—preparing to charge into battle.

Nothing in all the world compared to the beauty of a white horse. Why Uncle Antonio had never bought one I could never figure out.

But at least there were horses, and tomorrow I would get to see them. So as I fell asleep that night curled up tightly on the bottom bunk in Jaime's small, cramped bedroom, I tried hard to think about the horses and not about the miserable summer I was about to have.

CHAPTER 2

The White Horse

I rose bright and early—before anyone else had a chance to stir. (On a farm, you *have* to get up early if you want to beat everyone else up.) I pulled on my favorite orange shirt and found some old, faded cut-offs to wear. (I didn't bother putting on shoes because I preferred to go barefoot.) Then I slipped out of the room as quietly as possible, closed the front door behind me, and began making my way over to the barn.

I'd always loved mornings, even though I wasn't a "morning person." The air is so crisp in the morning (especially on a farm) and the birds are just beginning to sing. What I liked most about them, though, was the sky. If you make it outside before dawn, you can actually get to see the sun come peeking over the horizon. Before it does, though, the sky prepares for it a beautiful array of colors: First, it's mostly pink and blue. Then a few minutes later, a hint of orange and yellow begin to appear. And then—just as orange and yellow are giving way to purple and green—you begin to see a brilliant, pink sun deciding to make its way over to your side of the world. I felt lucky this morning to get to see it arriving on my side of the world.

I silently made my way towards the corral where the horses were kept. It was still dark outside, so I was careful to watch my step on the dusty dirt road. When I reached the corral gate, I climbed up a couple of wooden boards to my regular look-out spot and called to the horses. The dappled gray, named Big Thunder for his size, walked over to me and gently nudged my hand with his nose. Big Thunder was my favorite.

"Hey, boy," I smiled, patting his nose. "How're you doin'?" He pricked his ears in response.

I scratched his nose. There's no greater feeling in the world than the feeling you get when a horse lets you scratch its nose.

My arms soon grew tired of clinging to the wooden gate; I looked around for something else to stand on. An old tin water bucket was lying on the ground not far away. I brought it over to where I was (and to where three horses had now gathered), turned it upside down, and climbed on top of it. The horses, of course, wanted food, but—seeing as I had nothing to give them—they would have to be content with a scratch on the nose.

I looked toward the eastern horizon. The sun would be coming up soon. Already, the sky was beginning to change colors in that direction. (One advantage to being in a place where there aren't many trees is that you can enjoy an unobstructed view of the coming sun.) It wouldn't be long now.

It was so quiet and peaceful out here. I sighed; this might very well be the last chance I would have this summer to be alone with the horses.

I felt Big Thunder's mindful nudge on my hand— reminding me of his presence. I smiled and went back to my job of pacifying the horses' need for attention.

A few minutes later, I turned back to the horizon: A bright, pink sun was just beginning to show its face.

Suddenly, a terrible, high-pitched scream hit my ears. It startled me so badly that I lost my balance on the water bucket and fell over backwards onto the ground. I sat there for a couple minutes—trying to catch my breath and figure out what I had just heard. It had sounded like a horse's scream—you know, the sound a horse makes when it's startled or angry. But I had never heard *any* of Uncle Antonio's horses sound like that—not even Big Thunder! I looked up from the ground to see which of the horses had made the noise. The horses all appeared to be unflustered—as if they hadn't even *heard* the sound. I understood horses well enough to know that if they had heard what I heard, they wouldn't just be standing there stock still; they would be acting skittish, at the very least.

Slowly and carefully, I stood to my feet, turned the bucket over (it had, of course, become overturned as a result of my fall), and climbed back up. The horses were still there waiting for me to stroke their noses—wondering why I had stopped. I still didn't know what I had heard, but I decided that I wouldn't let it bother me. Like I said before, it does absolutely no good to worry about something that you can't do anything about.

Just as I had begun to think that it had only been my imagination (and that maybe I didn't get enough sleep last night), I heard the sound again. I needn't have bothered fixing the water bucket, because my next fall only overturned it once again. I looked up from the ground; standing before me—only a few yards away—was something I had only seen in my most beautiful dreams: a magnificent white horse.

Now, if this had been an *ordinary* white horse, it would have been enough. But only one look and anybody could see that this was no ordinary white horse. For one thing, it was *huge*—practically the size of an elephant! For another thing, an ordinary white horse wasn't this white; even though the sun had just barely risen over the horizon, the horse was so white that I found myself having to squint in order to look at it. (If the sun had been fully up, I probably would have been blinded.) And *every inch* of it was white—from the tip of its nose to the end of its tail; even its *hoofs* were white! The only part of the horse that wasn't white was its eyes, and these frightened me more than anything else. They burned red-hot, like two coals in a fire—and they were looking at *me!*

I sat there on the ground, petrified. I didn't know what the gigantic creature would do, but I knew that it was capable of trampling me without much effort at all. I held my breath and tried not to move a muscle, so as not to scare it. If this horse was jumpy in the least bit, I didn't want to frighten it into attacking me.

But the horse didn't move; it continued to stand there, motionless. I had never seen a horse stand this still before. Its enormous muscles didn't quiver, and its long mane and tail didn't blow in the breeze—even though there was a slight breeze this morning. It was as if nothing could touch it.

I wished *I* could touch it. Suddenly, as if in response to my thought, the horse started towards me! It didn't meander like most horses do—walking casually with its head bobbing up and down with every step. This horse walked *directly* over to me—keeping its massive head held high all the way.

It came within a few feet of me and stopped. I looked up at its face. The eyes were so powerful. There was something irresistible about them—as if they were drawing me to it. I wanted to run for my life, but at the same time I found myself wanting to be even nearer to it than I already was. Suddenly, a crazy idea popped into my head: *I want to ride it,* I thought.

Again, as if the horse had heard me, it stepped to the side with one swift, smooth motion—turning so that its left side was facing me. At first I was confused (and a little frightened) by this maneuver. Then I understood: anyone who's ever ridden a horse at least once or twice knows that the left side of a horse is the side used for mounting and dismounting. It almost appeared as though this horse were *asking* me to mount it!

I stood to my feet. I was dwarfed by the horse's enormous size; its back was two or three feet taller than the top of my head! How I'd even *imagined* I would ride it I didn't know. Even if I *did* find a way to climb up onto its back, its body was so huge that I wouldn't be able to stay on it for two seconds—not without a saddle, anyway.

I looked up at the fire-red eyes. Again, I felt that unmistakable desire to be closer. The eyes seemed to be saying to me, *"Come on, let's go."*

I looked around for the bucket I had used to stand on earlier. It was right in front of me—already resting in an upside-down position at the horse's side.

How did it get there? Hadn't I overturned it when I fell off of it only minutes ago?

I didn't have much time to consider the question, because I had already looked once again at the fiery eyes and was presently climbing onto the bucket, grabbing a hold of the long, flowing mane, and jumping with all my might onto its back.

CHAPTER 3

The Ride

The next thing I knew, I was racing down the dirt road at fifty miles an hour.

"Whoa!" I cried over and over. "Whoa!"

But the horse didn't seem to hear. It only continued on, faster and faster.

It was all I could do to hang on. I held tight to its mane, but I knew that I wouldn't be able to hold on much longer. Even though I was a pretty experienced rider, I had never ridden without a saddle and bridle before—and *never* on a horse of this size.

"Whoa!" I tried pulling at the mane to make it stop, but the horse didn't seem to feel a thing.

Under normal conditions, this would have been the highlight of my life; I'd always dreamed of riding a white horse. But under the present circumstances, I found myself just trying to survive.

For what seemed like an eternity, all I could see was white. Then there was a break in the whiteness as its mane parted and I could see something up ahead. What was it? It looked like we were fast approaching a wall, but it was so far away and I was bouncing around on top of the horse so much that I couldn't be sure.

Then I knew: A few years ago, Uncle Antonio had a fence built around the farm so that if any of his horses ever escaped the barn, they wouldn't be able to get too far away. He had it built extra high because some of the horses were excellent jumpers.

Was this horse going to try and jump it?

I panicked and began to yank at its mane to try and get it to turn. If the horse attempted to jump that fence and failed, neither I nor the horse would likely survive the fall. I pulled with all my might, but it was no use. The creature seemed to have a mind of its own, and it didn't seem to concern itself too much with my wishes.

Just as I had determined that the horse was going to jump—and had grabbed an extra-tight hold of the mane, shutting my eyes tight—I heard a strange sound. It sounded like a giant wind or rushing water.

I opened my eyes, then closed and opened them again to make sure I was seeing correctly. There, above my head to my right, was a gigantic, feathery, white wing! I looked over my left shoulder; an enormous white wing was on that side, too—presently flapping up and down.

Before the fact that I was riding atop a horse with wings had a chance to fully sink in, I felt myself being lifted off the ground. I closed my eyes tight and waited for the inevitable: the sensation of falling. I waited for several seconds—but it never came. Finally, I dared to open my eyes and look: The ground was miles and miles below.

We were flying!

This time, I didn't even try to understand it. I did what my instincts told me to do: I threw my arms out and yelled at the top of my lungs. At the time, it didn't seem to matter that I had just let go of the horse's mane and was now thousands of feet from the ground without holding on to anything. All that mattered was that my dreams were finally coming true right before my eyes.

Without warning, the horse suddenly folded its wings and dropped. I was in such a state of ecstasy that this move didn't even bother me. I wasn't afraid of heights, and already I had begun to trust the white horse beneath me. (I *did* decide to go ahead and grab a hold of the mane, though—just for extra measure.) We plummeted towards the Earth at a breath-taking rate. I thought we were going to hit the ground, but then the horse pulled up and headed for the sky again. I found that my feet were wet. I looked down below: The horse had come so close to a small lake that it had grazed the surface of the lake with one of its hoofs.

I laughed out loud. "You're showing off now," I said. "Let's see what else you can do."

As if accepting the challenge, the winged horse again folded its wings and dropped. This time, I heard its hoofs hit something that sounded like shingles on a roof. It *was* shingles on a roof! I laughed. The people inside the house were probably wondering why they had reindeer on the roof in the middle of the summer.

We climbed higher and higher—above the clouds. I could look down now and see not houses and lakes but miles and miles of clouds. If you've ever ridden in an airplane (I never had, as you may recall) and looked out the window, you might have seen what looks like snow stretched out for miles down below. Of course, it isn't really snow at all; it's clouds. But it looks so much like snow that you wish you could jump right out of the airplane and go run and play in the swirls of white. That's how it was for me now: I wished I could play in the snow-clouds.

I felt the horse lower itself a bit. I turned around on the horse and looked behind us: Four long, wide furrows were trailing us in the snow-clouds below. At first I was confused as to where they were coming from. Then I figured it out: They were being formed from the horse's giant hoofs as they dragged through the clouds. The horse was playing in the "snow"!

"I want to play, too!" I shouted. The horse lowered itself even more so that I could run *my* feet through the clouds. (The horse was nearly up to its neck in clouds now.) I laughed as the clouds tickled my toes like millions of soft, tiny flowers.

Without warning, the horse dropped—folding its wings only part-way this time so that we dropped only a little ways. I found myself momentarily down below with the snow-clouds right above my head. Then the horse's wings opened back up and we rose back to our former position. *I had just passed right through a cloud!* Before I could even catch my breath, the horse dropped and rose again with the ease of a tiny sparrow. Over and over again we dipped in and out of the snow-clouds—like being on the world's greatest roller coaster (without all the quick turns and uncomfortable bumps).

Now we left the snow-clouds behind and began to climb higher and higher into the sea of blue. I was surprised to find that—even at this high altitude (we must have been higher up than airplanes can fly!)—I didn't feel at all short of breath. Instead, I felt at peace—completely and totally at peace. In fact, I didn't know how I would ever be able to return to normal life after this. Maybe I wouldn't have to. Maybe I could find a way to stay up here forever.

I looked ahead. What was that in the far distance? It looked like a star, but why would a star be in the sky during the day? Maybe it was the morning star (it *was* morning, after all). It was very bright—brighter than any star I had ever seen before.

We were flying straight towards it; the horse seemed to have the light in mind as its destination. The closer we got to it, the brighter the light became. I shielded my eyes with the back of my hand. Suddenly, the light was all around us, and I couldn't see a thing.

CHAPTER 4

Mensajero

The next thing I remember is feeling two large hands lifting me from the horse and setting me on the ground. One of the hands touched my eyes and I found that I could see again. (The bright light must have temporarily blinded me.) I blinked a couple times then looked to see who had lifted me from the horse. I blinked again. Standing before me was the tallest man I had ever seen in my life. Or was it a man? I had never seen a man with wings before.

He was very handsome—clean-shaven and skin the color of bronze. The robe that he wore was dazzlingly white, like the horse. I couldn't see his arms very well because they were hidden beneath the robe, but even so I could tell that the man was extremely strong. A wide, golden sash was draped diagonally across his chest from his shoulder to the golden belt tied around his waist. Attached to the belt was a sheath—so long that it nearly touched the ground—with a sword inside. The sword's hilt was beautifully crafted gold (apparently, gold was the man's favorite thing to wear), and the man's left hand was resting on the hilt of the sword. The feathery white wings on his back were as tall as he was—arching up over his head about a foot and hanging about a foot off the ground.

The ground. What was I standing on? I looked down at my feet: It looked and felt surprisingly similar to the snow-clouds I had run my feet through earlier. Was I actually standing on a cloud?

I must be dreaming, I thought.

"Welcome to Paraíso, little one," I heard a strong, kind voice say.

I looked up at the man's face. I was only about half his height (he must have been close to nine feet tall!), so looking up at the man's face was not easy. The eyes that met mine scared me nearly as much as the horse's had. They were blue—but not like any shade of blue I had ever seen in a person's eyes before. They were the color of sapphire, and they shone as if they really *were* made of sapphire. It would be easy to get lost in those eyes, I thought, and forget about everything else.

That must have been what happened because the next thing I knew the man was kneeling down in front of me on one knee. "Welcome to Paraíso," he said again. His face was like his voice—strong and kind. I noticed that his left hand never left the hilt of his sword.

I must have looked scared to death because he presently said, "You need not be afraid, little one. No harm will come to you. And this sword is meant only for outsiders." I hoped I wasn't an outsider. "Have you come to enter the Kingdom of Paraíso today as a special guest or as a permanent resident?"

I didn't know. I didn't even know what I was doing here in the first place—or if I even *was* here or just dreaming the whole thing up. I found that all I could think about was the size of this guy and how powerful he looked.

"I was told by the King earlier today to expect a special guest," the man continued courteously despite my lack of response. "Perhaps you are the one to whom he was referring.

What is your name, little one?"

My name? I had a name? Yes, I probably did. Now, what was it again?

It must have taken me a full minute to think of it. The man waited patiently for it to come to me. "Sara," I finally managed to whisper.

"Sara," he smiled gently, "—the title of a princess. Welcome to the Kingdom of Paraíso, Sara. I am called Mensajero—the King's messenger. My occupation is to deliver messages given me by the King, and to defend the King's subjects. On this special day, however, it would appear as though a new job has been assigned to me: the job of greeting one of Paraíso's special guests!" He gave me a wink.

I tried to smile, but I couldn't stop shaking. His eyes frightened me—and they strangely reminded me of Aunt Sarah's, somehow.

"Fear not, little one," he said, gently placing his large right hand on my shoulder.

For some reason, I suddenly stopped shaking and felt much more calm. He smiled and removed his hand from my shoulder. Then he did something strange: he took both of my hands in both of his and gently turned me so that I was no longer facing him. He sat there for a moment in silence—staring straight ahead in the direction I was now facing, still holding on to my hands. I looked down; his hands looked so powerful . . . and yet gentle—and they completely engulfed mine. I looked at his eyes, but his gaze could not be diverted from whatever held his attention. I wondered whether or not he was going to say anything else. I hoped he would; the silence was making me uncomfortable. Finally, he let go with his right hand and pointed out in front of him. "Do you see the Great Palace in the distance?"

I followed his gesture. In the distance was a bright light—almost like a sun but much larger and much brighter; in fact, I couldn't look at it for any time before having to look away. It reminded me very much of the bright light I had seen while riding atop the great white horse. I didn't see the "Great Palace" he was talking about, but I nodded anyway.

He clasped both of my hands again and slowly turned me back to face him. "Sara," he said in a more serious tone of voice and with a more serious expression on his face, "it is in that Palace where the King of Paraíso dwells. Paraíso is his throne, and the Earth is his footstool. The light you see is the King's glory. He dwells there with his Son, the Prince of Paraíso—blessed be his name forever and ever!" He unexpectedly flapped his wings—creating an enormous wind that would have knocked me over had he not had a tight hold of my hands. "Here in the Kingdom of Paraíso," he continued, "we have no need for moon or sun or stars. Our source of light is the Prince of Paraíso himself—as he is for all who know him." He paused for a moment, gazing at the light. Then he looked at me: his eyes seemed brighter. "Do you yet know the King and his Son on a personal basis?"

On a personal basis? How could I know them at all since I'd never been here before? I shook my head.

I saw something like sadness fill his eyes, and he turned away. After a long time I heard him say, "That *is* a shame. But there is still time." He looked at me and his smile returned. "Yes," he said in a brighter voice. "Yes, of *course* there is still time! But our time *today* is running short: You must return quickly to your own world, Sara, in order to fulfill the Great Commission. You still have much left to do and much left to see. But, come, there is still much to be done and even more to be seen on *this* day! I must go at once and inform the King of your arrival (although I feel certain he already knows) so that he may appoint a host to guide you on a short tour of Paraíso. It will have to be a short tour, mind you, for Espíritu returns in haste for those whom he has chosen. You are familiar with Espíritu, I assume?"

I shook my head.

"It is Espíritu who made possible today your trip to the Great City."

The horse? Was he talking about the horse? I wouldn't say I was *familiar* with it, but I *had* taken a rather breathtaking ride on it earlier this morning on my way to the "Great City." (Why did everything have to be "Great"?)

"Espíritu is a wonderful comforter and a wise teacher," the man with wings continued. "You would do well to get to know him better. I must go now, little one. A host will be sent to you shortly to show you around the Great City. Please feel the freedom to walk around and enjoy yourself before your host arrives. Paraíso boasts many beautiful sites. And I *do* hope, Sara, to make your acquaintance here again in the future."

He looked so serious, as if he expected a response. But I didn't know what to say, (which had been the case for most of today), so I nodded. Then he did something that surprised me very much. The powerful man released my hands and wrapped his muscular arms around me in a hug. He held me close—so close, in fact, that the velvety feathers from one of his wings brushed against my cheek. (He knew his own strength, thank goodness, so he was careful not to squeeze me too tightly.) After holding me like that for what seemed like an eternity, he finally let me go. Then he stood to his feet, looked at me one last time, did an about-face (his left hand returning to the hilt of his sword), and began walking in the direction of the bright light. In what seemed like no time at all, he was gone from view.

CHAPTER 5

Paraíso

Now alone, my head began to clear. I still wasn't sure I wasn't dreaming, but I was beginning to think that I wasn't. Everything was too real. The clouds beneath my feet—the . . . what was above my head? It wasn't sky. It looked like gold, and there were no clouds or sun. Indeed, the only light in this "Great City" seemed to originate from the bright light in the distance.

I looked around me. To my left were fruit trees completely covered with fruits of all kinds. When I say that the trees were covered with fruits of all kinds, I don't mean that there were all kinds of fruit trees—each tree was the same. What I mean is that there were all different kinds of fruit on *each tree!* Most trees bear only one kind of fruit; the ones I was presently looking at bore *many* different kinds: apples, oranges, bananas, pears, blueberries, grapes, cherries, peaches, strawberries . . . what were the others? I didn't recognize the others. I counted them up: each tree had *twelve* different kinds of fruit growing on it! *That's convenient,* I thought. *If you don't like one kind of fruit, you're sure to like another.* And the fruits weren't like ordinary fruits, either; they glowed like lights on a Christmas tree.

But what amazed me even more than this was where the trees appeared to be growing: right out of a golden street! And I don't mean a gold-colored street; the street was made entirely out of *pure gold!* And coursing right down the middle of the wide, golden street—alongside the rows of trees—was a river of the purest, most beautiful, most refreshing-looking water I had ever seen. It sparkled as brilliantly as the golden street through which it streamed. (I couldn't be sure, but as I stopped to listen to the gently flowing waters, I almost thought I could hear the sound of sweet music playing.) Both the river and the golden street seemed to lead to (or flow *from*) that bright light in the distance—which, apparently, was the King's Palace.

On either side of the street were rows and rows of the most spectacular mansions I had ever seen in my life. They were immaculate and immense—constructed entirely out of precious stones, including both diamonds and rubies. "Who lives *there*?" I wondered aloud. "*More* kings and queens?"

Just then, one of the mansion doors opened and a child ran out. It was a little boy with a shining face around the age of seven or eight. I watched as he closed the door behind him and ran over to one of the neighboring mansions— knocking loudly on the door. The door opened and another boy answered the door. (Did these kids *live* in those mansions?) They talked for a minute, but I was too far away to be able to hear what they were saying. The boy who had answered the door ran back inside his "house" and returned a few minutes later wearing a different shirt. Then both boys ran down the main street to all the other mansions—knocking on all the doors and talking to those who lived there until quite a collection of children had gathered on the golden street. (Those who lived across the street—and across the river—were reached by way of a golden bridge linking the two sides.) The children then proceeded to run as a group to a nearby field where they began to play a game I had never seen before. It looked like a combination of dodge ball and a snowball fight—except that nobody got hurt and nobody got out.

After a few minutes of playing, one of the girls spotted me (I don't know how since she was so far away) and started running in my direction. "Hi," she said enthusiastically when she had reached me, sweeping her long, black hair away from her face. "Would you like to come play with us?"

I looked at the girl. She was about my age, maybe a little younger—but she looked older, too, somehow. She had dark eyes and hair, just like me. In fact, I was a little surprised by how much she resembled me. (She was much prettier than me, though.) She was grinning from ear to ear. "Please join us," she said, hardly able to control her excitement.

"I—I don't know," I said.

"Come on," she urged, grabbing a hold of my arm and starting to pull me in that direction. "You can be on my team. You're already dressed for it and everything."

I pulled away from her and looked down at what I was wearing: just a t-shirt and shorts. I looked at the kids; the game *did* look fun.

"How do you play it?" I asked.

The girl looked surprised. "You've never played it?" she asked.

I shook my head.

"I thought *everyone* who lived in the Kingdom of Paraíso knew how to play Nieve-nube."

I raised an eyebrow at the strange name. "I don't *live* in the Kingdom of Paraíso," I responded.

For a moment, the girl looked confused. Then a surprised look came over her face and she appeared to be thinking about something. Her expression suddenly became one of excitement. "Of *course* you don't live here!" she exclaimed, again grabbing my arm and jumping up and down and laughing as if I had just told the funniest joke in the world. "Of *course* you don't live here—you're a special guest! Oh, please, please, you *have* to let me show you around Paraíso! But first, you have to learn how to play Nieve-nube—it's *loads* of fun! Come on!"

Before I could object, the girl had grabbed my arm (she was a lot stronger than she looked!) and pulled me over to the field and to the group of children. The field was white—as if it were made of clouds. It probably was.

"There are two teams," the girl said, quickly explaining the rules, "and everyone lines up on opposite ends of the field. When the scorekeeper yells 'Go!', everyone picks up a handful of cloud and tries to hit the other team with it. (Don't worry—the snow-clouds don't hurt like snowballs do. It feels kind of like being hit by a big powder-ball!) If a snow-cloud hits you, it will turn your shirt white. (Everyone starts out with a shirt that isn't white. Today, as you can see, the two colors we've decided on are orange and blue. The shirt you're wearing is *perfect!*) If your shirt turns white, you're still in the game; you just keep throwing snow-clouds at those whose shirts aren't white yet. The first team to turn all of the other team's shirts white wins. Are you ready for your first round of Nieve-nube?"

I looked at the kids; the two teams were presently shaking out their shirts (presumably getting the snow-clouds off of them) and taking their places in line—gathering up handfuls of cloud. The girl and I took our places on the orange side since she was a member of the orange team and since, ironically, I was already wearing an orange shirt.

"Ready!" the scorekeeper (who was a boy with red hair and freckles) yelled. "Get set! GO!!"

Everyone ran up to the line dividing the two teams and took their best shot. I looked down at my feet. The entire field consisted of the snow-clouds, so I wouldn't have to worry about running out of ammunition. I bent down and scooped up a handful of cloud. It felt like snow except that it wasn't freezing cold and it was much simpler and faster to make into a ball. *I must be dreaming,* I thought to myself. *I'm standing here holding a snowball made out of cloud.*

Suddenly, I felt something hit me in the chest with a dull splattering sound. I looked down: My orange shirt had a huge white spot on the front of it. I looked up to see a boy cheering at his "direct hit."

I bunched up the snow-cloud I was holding into a tighter ball, took aim, and got the boy on the arm. "Hey!" I heard him say with a laugh and watched as he quickly formed a new ball in his hands. I ducked right as the snow-cloud whizzed over my head.

"Ha, ha!" I called. "You missed m—" But I didn't get to finish my sentence because someone else's snow-cloud had hit me in the mouth. I was mad until I realized with amazement that it hadn't hurt at all and that the snow-cloud tasted surprisingly similar to powdered sugar. I was just about to reach down and grab another handful to stuff in my mouth when an unidentified snow-cloud hit me on the shoulder.

The battle was on. I found myself an adept player of Nieve-nube because I had the advantage of being the pitcher of a baseball team back home, and I could throw some pretty mean balls. The best part, of course, was that nobody got hurt, and so nobody got mad. (In fact, getting hit was a pleasure if the snow-cloud happened to hit you in the mouth.) It was all laughs and giggles and smiles—something I hadn't experienced in a long time. I was actually disappointed when—after a long while (because, after all, it takes a long time to turn the entire surface of somebody's shirt white)—the score-keeper called out "Orange wins!" and everybody cheered because either their team won or their friends' team won. As both teams celebrated, I realized for the first time that there were children of all nationalities gathered here: Hispanics, Blacks, Whites, Indians, Asians—

you name it, they were there. And they . . . I mean, *we* . . .
were all having fun together.

In the midst of the celebration, the dark-haired girl
approached me. "You did *great!*" she laughed, brushing the
snow-cloud from my shirt. "I *knew* you'd enjoy it! I wish
you could stay for another game, but Espíritu will be here
soon to pick you up and you haven't even seen the *best* of
Paraíso. Follow me!"

And then, as if I had no choice in the matter (because,
really, I didn't), I was whisked away with the girl holding
tight to my hand—the both of us running so fast we nearly
flew. I looked over my shoulder to see another round of
Nieve-nube about to begin.

CHAPTER 6

The Book of Life

When we'd stopped running and the girl let go of my hand, I was surprised to find myself not out of breath. My breath was taken away, though, when I saw what was before me: A giant golden staircase, seemingly suspended in midair, extended upwards into the "sky" so high that I couldn't even see the top of it. Armed guards with wings and swords lined the staircase—all of them with their left hands resting on the hilts of their swords.

"This," the dark-haired girl explained, "is the most important place in Paraíso—besides the Palace, of course." She took my hand again and pulled me over to the staircase. A few of the guards near the base of the staircase drew their swords. "It's okay," the girl said quickly. "She's with me."

I watched as they slowly and cautiously sheathed their swords—keeping their eyes focused on me. "Let's go!" the girl said excitedly, taking off again and dragging me up the staircase. All the way to the top, I could feel the watchful eyes of the guards on me.

When we'd finally reached the top (it didn't take nearly as long to get there as it should have), I found myself on a large platform with winged armed guards keeping watch all around the perimeter. In the center was a tall podium with the largest book I had ever seen in my life resting on top of it. Surrounding the podium were four more guards. The book was closed, and the words of some foreign language were written on the cover.

"That's the Book of Life," the girl said. "It's a sacred Book—written before the foundation of the world. This is as close as we can get to it; but, really, it wouldn't do us much good to be any closer anyway."

"Why?" I asked.

"Because we can't open it," she explained. "Only the King can open it, and he won't do that until the end of the world when the list of names will be read off. Written in that Book are the names of every person who ever has—or ever *will*—come to live in Paraíso as a permanent resident." She paused. "Is *your* name in there?" she asked suddenly, turning to face me.

How did I know? "I—I'm not sure," I said, shrugging my shoulders. I figured that would be a safe answer. I was wrong.

"You'd *better* be sure," she said, her carefree demeanor changing to one of deep concern. "It's those who aren't sure who end up getting left out."

"Left out of what?" I asked.

"Left *out*," she said, grabbing me by the shoulders. "Left out of *this*." She made a sweeping motion with her arm. "Left out of paradise. Left out of *Paraíso*."

She stood there looking at me intently. I felt as though I should be feeling something, but I didn't know what to feel. "Well," I said, trying to break the awkward silence, "what happens if I get left out?"

With this, the girl grabbed my arm (I was getting a little tired of being dragged around) and pulled me over to the edge of the platform—at least as close as we could get to it without bumping into one of the armed guards. "Do you see that wall over there?" she said, pointing.

"What wall?" All I saw was gold about 50 yards away.

"Over there," she said, still pointing.

That was a wall? It stretched for miles and miles; I could see neither the end of it nor the beginning. I looked up; I couldn't see the top of it, either—not even from this height. I had thought that I was looking at the sky. Maybe the wall *did* reach the sky!

"That is one of the four walls enclosing Paraíso," said the girl. "Each wall is 1,400 miles high and 1,400 miles long, and each wall has three gates guarded by a criado. See? There's one of the gates over there."

Again she pointed. Far down below us was a gigantic gate—or *would* have been a gigantic gate if I had been up close. Just the fact that I could see it from this height, though, meant that it must have been of considerable size. The gate looked beautiful—shining brightly like a pearl.

"You can't see the criado from this distance, but he's down there," she said.

"What's a criado?" I asked.

The girl laughed. Had I said something funny? "Criados are the King's servants who defend the King's people and deliver his messages," she answered. "They also help to protect important things like the Book of Life." She pointed to the guards standing right in front of us. "These guys here are criados," she said. I hoped they weren't listening.

"Not only does a criado stand guard at each of the twelve gates," the girl continued, "but the walls themselves are extremely thick—216 feet! That's wide enough for 36 cars to drive along the top of it side-by-side!"

"Wow," I said in amazement. "Why does it need to be so thick?"

The girl took my arm and pulled me back to the center of the platform, her face becoming very grave. "That's what

I've been leading up to," she said with a darker tone. "You wanted to know what happens if you get left out of the Kingdom of Paraíso. There's a place on the other side of that wall called the Land of Lamento. Picture in your mind (if you can) a place as terrible as Paraíso is wonderful and you'll understand a *fraction* of what Lamento is like. It's a literal living death for all who live there. The people in Lamento would do *anything* to be able to cross over to Paraíso. That's why the walls are so thick—to keep people in Lamento from being able to get in. Not that they could really get anywhere near the walls, anyway; there's a giant chasm separating the two places." The girl paused for a minute and shuddered. "It's an awful place—the Land of Lamento," she said in a strange voice. "Darkness forever. A fire that never goes out. Worms that feed on you." This time *I* shuddered. "If you get left out, you go to Lamento."

I was beginning to feel a little queasy; I was afraid I was going to be sick when suddenly the girl's bright expression returned and she said excitedly, "But here's the *good* news: *No one has to be left out!* In fact, it's quite easy to guarantee your place here in the Kingdom of Paraíso! All you have to do is love the King and follow him, and believe in his Son, the Prince."

I was shocked. "If it's that easy," I said, "then why does *anyone* get left out?"

"That," she answered sadly, "is a question I've never quite been able to answer. It is a mystery that will never be solved—in my mind, anyway. The best I can tell, the reason why most people get left out is because they don't want to have to follow the King. They would rather live life their own way and not have to answer to anyone. What they don't realize is that *only* by serving the King can they ever experience true freedom. It's like they're on an endless search for something they'll never find in a place they'll never find it— when only they have to look to Paraíso and see the King."

I felt somehow that the girl was saying something significant, even though I didn't understand it all. I understood the part about wanting to live life your own way; I didn't much like people telling me what to do.

"But you," the girl said suddenly, grabbing hold of my hand and grinning from ear to ear. "*You* realize the truth! *You* understand that serving the King brings freedom, so you don't have a *thing* to worry about!"

This girl's perky attitude was starting to get on my nerves, and I *didn't* like how she was constantly touching me (I wasn't a touchy-feely type person). And besides that, I couldn't get a word in edgewise. "Why should I have to obey and serve *your* King?" I demanded, jerking my hand away. "After all, he's not the King where *I* come from."

"Oh, but he is!" the girl exclaimed, overlooking my obvious annoyance of her. "He's the King of *both* worlds— mine *and* yours! Did you think Paraíso was the King's only concern? Most of his time is spent overseeing the activities of Earth. That's where his priorities lie—at least for now."

"Why?"

"You'll find out soon enough," she winked, "as soon as you return to your own world. Now that you have the Power of Paraíso, you'll be able to see the war for yourself."

"*What* war?" I insisted, becoming more frustrated by the second. "What are you *talking* about? And what in the world is 'the Power of Paraíso'?"

"Now that you have been to Paraíso," she explained calmly, "you will begin to see things from Paraíso's point of view. You will be able to see both the criados and the sombras (and, believe me, there are a *lot* of them!) for the first time ever. You will never have to wonder again why some things happen the way they do; the answer will be right before your eyes."

This conversation was making absolutely zero sense to me, and I was the kind of person who *had* to understand things or else I went crazy. "What if I choose not to believe *any* of this?" I asked defensively. "What if I choose to believe that not a single word you have said to me this entire time was even true? What if I choose to believe that Paraíso doesn't even exist—that this whole thing has been just a figment of my imagination . . . nothing but one long, meaningless dream?"

The girl looked me directly in the eyes. "If this is all a dream," she said to me, "then consider yourself about to be wakened."

CHAPTER 7

The Golden Key

The girl told me that she wanted to give me something, but that we would have to go back to her house to get it. "Come on," she said, taking me by the hand. "Let's go!" And off we flew.

Oh, brother, I thought. *Here we go again.*

I was glad when once we had reached the bottom of the staircase she stopped running and we were able to walk along at a leisurely pace. I wanted to be able to take in the view around me. *This* must *be a dream,* I decided. *Everything is too beautiful.*

Surrounding us on both sides were trees. They were the most gorgeous trees I had ever seen; their long, thick limbs spread out in all directions (they would have made great climbing trees, I thought), and their leaves—like nearly everything else here—sparkled like gold. On a few of the trees, green, leafy vines wound their way around the trunks. The trees were dispersed at intervals so that it almost appeared as though someone had carefully planted them in such a way so as to make sure no tree would grow up too close or too far away from another. The squirrels that ran about them were able to leap from tree to tree without ever touching the ground. Not that the squirrels seemed to *mind* touching the ground; the mossy, green turf was littered with hundreds of apparently delicious-tasting nuts of which many of the squirrels were freely partaking. (Once, one of the squirrels ran right up to me; I was amazed when it actually allowed me to bend down and stroke its back and its soft, fluffy tail.) Countless birds also inhabited the trees—all of them bright, brilliant colors. Their song was so peaceful that I found myself wondering whether it was truly the birds that were creating the sound or if a symphony orchestra was playing somewhere nearby.

Beyond the trees were mountains of gigantic proportions—towering so high that I couldn't even see the tops of many of them. And yet there was no snow on them, not even near the top. They were luscious and green, and when they weren't green they were purple—sparkling like jewels. Below one of the mountains was a crystal-clear pool where the water from a giant waterfall was gathering. I couldn't be sure, but I thought I saw a child jump from one of the mountain cliffs into the pool.

"The water is warm," said the girl, following my gaze. "Good for swimming year round."

Something about this girl still annoyed me. I tried to think of a reason to be mad at her. "You never told me your name," I said, glaring at her.

"You never asked," she laughed. It seemed nothing could faze her. "It's Risa," she said, rolling the "r" as she said the word.

"Whoa!" I laughed, in spite of myself. "It's *what?*"

"R-r-r-risa!" she repeated, laughing even harder than before.

I couldn't help but laugh myself. "How did you *do* that?" I asked.

"It's not difficult to learn how with a little practice,"

she winked.

There was a pause. A couple of squirrels scampered across our cloud-covered path in a game of tag. "It's a pretty name," I said quietly, watching as the squirrels scurried up a nearby tree.

"Thank you," she smiled. "It's the name I was given when I came to live in Paraíso. Everyone who comes to live in Paraíso as a permanent resident is given a white stone with his or her new name carved on it. Risa is the new name I received."

"What was your old name?" I wondered.

"I don't really recall," she said, tilting her head to the side. "I don't remember much at *all* about my old life; it's almost like a dream, you know? I remember parts of it sometimes, but only the good parts. As hard as I've tried, I can't seem to remember anything bad. But, really," she laughed, "why should I want to remember anything bad anyway?"

I looked at her. Maybe the atmosphere of this new place was starting to have an effect on me, but I decided that maybe the girl was okay. She was still annoying, but—

"What is that on your forehead?" I nearly shouted, stopping her in her tracks.

At first she looked surprised at my alarm, then she gave her typical response and laughed. "Oh, that," she chuckled. "Don't be afraid—it's another name. It's the name of the King. Everyone who comes to live in Paraíso also gets the King's name inscribed on their forehead."

"Oh," I said, a little embarrassed by my reaction. "Well, why didn't I notice it there before?"

Risa smiled. "The Power of Paraíso must be kicking in," she said.

We were presently approaching the neighborhood of mansions. It looked as though the game of Nieve-nube was still in full force. "Wait here," Risa said excitedly and ran quickly over to a mansion made mostly of rubies. I watched the children as they played. I watched as the blue team won a round.

"Here it is!" Risa called, running back to me. She took my hand and placed in it a large golden key. "This key is to the greatest treasure in the world," she grinned.

I turned it over in my hand. It was so bright it almost seemed to glow.

"Your world is a dark one," she continued. "This key will help lead you to the light."

Just then, one of the girls from the orange team ran over to us. She said something to Risa in another language.

"Okay, I'll be there in just a couple minutes," Risa answered.

The girl said something else, smiled at me, then ran back to the game.

"How in the world did you understand her?" I asked in amazement. "It sounded like she was speaking Chinese."

"She was!" Risa laughed. "She used to live in Taiwan before coming to live here. In Taiwan, her family spoke Mandarin Chinese. Everyone in Paraíso speaks the language they were used to speaking on Earth, so there are *many* different languages spoken in the Kingdom of Paraíso. I don't know how we can all understand each other, but we can. For example, I knew that Dulce (that's the name of the girl that was just here—the one who was speaking Chinese) was asking me to come back and join in the game (which I will do just as soon as I finish speaking with you) even though I don't know Mandarin Chinese. Pretty neat, huh?"

Up until now, I hadn't cared much for foreign languages. But I had to admit that this was pretty cool.

"Here he comes," Risa said, pointing towards the sky.

I looked up. Far in the distance, I could barely make out the shape of a winged horse headed our way.

"I wish you didn't have to leave so soon," Risa said sadly, "but when Espíritu comes for you, you're best advised to go with him."

"I never told you my name," I said quickly, stuffing the golden key into my shorts pocket. "It's Sara."

"Sara," the girl repeated thoughtfully. "That's a pretty name. It seems familiar to me, somehow. I must have known a Sara in my former life," she laughed.

Espíritu had flown quickly and was already on the ground awaiting my arrival. It was looking at me with those piercing red eyes.

"Bye, Risa," I said, then hesitated. "I know I didn't say your name right," I confessed.

She burst into laughter. "That's okay," she smiled. "You practice rolling your 'r's, and maybe by the time we meet again you'll be able to say it!"

"I doubt it," I chuckled.

Espíritu stamped his foot.

I started for the horse, then went back and surprised myself by giving Risa a hug. I then ran and—grabbing a hold of Espíritu's mane—found myself miraculously able to jump onto its back.

"Good-bye, Sara," Risa called as I flew away. "Come back soon!"

CHAPTER 8

Espíritu

I guess I expected Espíritu to drop me off at Uncle Antonio's house—the same place he had picked me up. So when we landed near the entrance of a small church on the edge of town, I was a little surprised. For a minute I just sat there. I looked around me. I knew where I was; this was still Uncle's Antonio's town because I recognized this church as having driven past it many times on our way out of town. Uncle Antonio's house was not far away.

I tried to think of what to say. I first looked around me to make sure no one was looking. I didn't want someone to think I was strange for talking to a horse. (I suppose, however, that the sight of a girl talking to a horse would be only secondary to the sight of an elephant-sized horse with wings.)

I cleared my throat. "Espíritu," I began quietly and respectfully. (I didn't want to offend it, if it *could* be offended; I was still sitting on its back, after all.) "Espíritu, you got very close. Uncle Antonio's house is just a little ways that way."

Not surprisingly, the horse didn't respond.

I sighed. What was I *doing?* I had spoken to horses before—*many* times, on Uncle Antonio's farm—but I had never tried to *reason* with a horse before. I'd had enough experience with horses to know that this would be a point-less endeavor, as horses aren't the smartest creatures on four legs. With this in mind, I felt even more foolish as I contin-ued my prodding. "Espíritu," I said, losing more and more confidence in the sanity of this operation every minute, "the house is over that way." I even gave it a visual—turning around and pointing in the direction of the house. "*That* way, Espíritu," I said, louder this time, just in case it might be hard of hearing. "The house is over *that* way!"

Again, no response—not even a twitching of the ears. The horse merely stood there, still as a statue.

I was losing patience. I could get off of it and walk the rest of the way myself, but this option seemed pointless to me since I was riding a perfectly capable horse. Therefore, I did now what any other reasonable person would have done in my situation: I kicked it in the sides. This was a mistake. The giant horse reared up—emitting a terrible, high-pitched scream. I tumbled backwards off its back, rolling along the ground and nearly hitting my head against a tree. My head still spinning, I looked up from the ground at the amazing creature. I watched as it turned—slowly and majestically so that now I could see its face and it could see mine. The eyes burned like two hot coals in a fire. Surely this was no ordi-nary winged horse.

I stood to my feet. Is it possible to feel afraid and brave at the same time? That's how I felt now: scared to death and yet—since I was standing face to face with the most terrify-ing creature that ever lived—very brave.

As I continued to look at his face, I suddenly felt as though I was supposed to do something. I looked at the church. It was like most other churches I'd seen: a few stained-glass windows, big double doors, a steeple with a cross on top. It was a small church—probably no more than a couple hundred could fit inside. What purpose could such a church serve?

I looked back at Espíritu. Now that those eyes had looked upon me, I doubted whether I could ever be content to look anywhere else.

I walked over to the double doors. I tried opening them, but they were locked. I stopped to think. What day was today? It was Saturday. Of course they were locked—a church is never open on Saturday.

I turned around and looked at the horse. "It's closed, Espíritu," I said to him. "The doors are locked. I can't get in." Somehow I knew that getting into that church was Espíritu's assignment for me.

As I stood there looking at him, it suddenly occurred to me that I had not yet tried the eastern door. I went to look: sure enough, there was another door on the east side of the church. How could I have known that there was a door there? I'd never visited this church before. Where did the thought to "check the eastern door" come from? Maybe Espíritu had given it to me.

I tried the door. It too was locked.

Again I walked back to Espíritu. "It's locked, too," I said. "Do you know of another door I could try?" I waited for an idea of another door to come to me. Instead, a different thought entered my mind: the key Risa had given me. I had not yet tried to use the golden key.

I reached into my pocket. *The key was gone!*

I panicked. I checked the other pocket—maybe I had stuffed it in there. It was empty, too!

I sat down on the front steps of the church and began to cry. I knew it was dumb to cry, but I couldn't help it. I'd been entrusted with the key to "the greatest treasure in the world" and I'd lost it. Maybe the treasure was right on the other side of that door. Now I would never know.

I was always messing things up. Just like when Mom died. I'd promised her I would take care of my dad. I hadn't. In fact, I'd probably just made his life worse. Before my mother died, at least he smiled once in a while. Now he hardly ever smiled. It was probably because of me. I was a disappointment to my dad. I had done something (I don't know what) to make him angry with me—that's why he was always in a bad mood. *That's* why he was so negative. It was because of me.

A high-pitched scream woke me from my thoughts. Through blurry eyes I saw Espíritu rearing high up on his hind legs—churning the air with his front. He looked so magnificent: wings outspread and beating the air like a swan on a crystal lake. For a moment I forgot all about my problems and simply gazed upon Espíritu.

Then a strange thing happened: A sensation came over me that everything was going to be okay. It didn't make sense; I knew that everything was *not* okay. And yet I felt at peace. Everything that was wrong could be made right somehow.

Just then, I heard a noise. I ran around to the side of the church: the eastern door was standing wide open.

I ran back to thank Espíritu, but he was already gone.

CHAPTER 9

The Church

I looked inside. The church was dark; no lights were on at all. From the light of the sun—although there wasn't much because it was evening (I guess I had spent the entire day in Paraíso) and the sun was on the opposite side of the building—I could tell that I was looking down a long hallway. It looked like I imagined it would: framed pictures on the walls, a small table with a lamp on it (the lamp was turned off), doorways along the sides that probably led to Sunday school classrooms. I didn't see anything out of the ordinary. I certainly didn't see "the greatest treasure in the world."

I considered what to do. I could just go home (I knew my way from here) and forget about finding the "treasure." The idea of walking through a dark church didn't exactly thrill me. I didn't much care for walking through a church at all—much less a dark one. But my curiosity had already gotten the best of me, and I stepped inside.

Up until now, I had never thought of church as being scary before. From my own experience, church was long, boring, and strict—but never scary. We used to go quite a bit—a long time ago, before my mother died. Ever since she died, though, we just sort of stopped going. I wasn't sure why. I asked my dad about it one time but he just said that church was for people like my mother, not for us, and for me to drop the matter. I never pursued it. After all, not going to church on Sunday meant that I could sleep later and not have to sit through a long, boring sermon. Church was a waste of time—unexciting and uneventful. But never scary.

Church was scary to me now. There wasn't a speck of light in this place, and I kept worrying that I would bump into something and knock something over. I walked along with my hands outstretched—groping along in the dark like a blind person. *This is ridiculous,* I thought to myself. *There is absolutely* no *point in my even being here. I should just leave.* But again the mystery of the unknown appealed to me and I continued on.

I came to what seemed to be a cross-section in which the hallway intersected with another. I stood there for a minute—trying to decide which way to go. Suddenly, I heard a noise. I had grown so accustomed to the complete silence of this place that it made me jump. I stood there frozen—my heart pounding in my chest. Was there someone else in the building besides me? What if they asked me what I was doing here? What would I say? Somehow "I'm here looking for the greatest treasure in the world" didn't sound like a very believable response.

I heard the sound again. It was a distant sound—like it was coming from a long ways away. What *was* it? It sounded like singing. Of course! It was Saturday—the church choir was probably here practicing for tomorrow's service.

I decided to turn right and walk in the direction of the sound. I didn't want to meet anybody, but at least if I went towards the sound I might find a bit of light in this place (I was tired of walking in the dark). The choir members surely would have turned some lights on when they entered the building.

The singing grew louder, so I knew I was getting close. But every time I would open a door, expecting to see people on the other side, the room would be completely dark. It was almost as if the singing were leading me on—remaining always just ahead of me but always just out of reach.

Finally, I encountered a room with double doors. The singing beyond these doors was louder than anywhere else I had encountered. *This must be the sanctuary,* I thought to myself. *Sanctuaries usually have double doors. Of all the rooms in a church, this is the one that is most likely to have a choir in it.* I paused for a moment, hypnotized by the music. *What a choir!* I mused. *If our choir back home sounded that good, I would show up on Sunday just to hear them sing!* Forget *sleeping late!*

But when I opened the door, I got the same result as before: total darkness. And the singing disappeared altogether.

"What *is* this?" I exclaimed, my angry voice echoing throughout the large, empty room. "I *know* I heard singing in here! Hello? Is there anybody in here?"

Silence.

This was maddening. I had heard that searching for buried treasure wasn't easy, but this was ridiculous.

I was just about to close the double doors back and leave the building once and for all when I saw a small speck of light. This was the first light I had seen anywhere thus far, so naturally I was curious. I felt the urge once again to leave the building—that this was all just a waste of time—but the pull of the unknown drove me forward. I entered the room and started for the light.

I walked slowly at first. Then my excitement over the fact that I had finally found some light got the better of me and I began to walk a little faster. My suspicion that this was a sanctuary was suddenly justified as I ran headlong into one of the wooden pews.

I crumbled to the floor in agony, holding my left knee. I bit my lip hard to keep from crying. "Stupid!" I scolded myself. "How stupid can you be? You *knew* there would be pews in here!" I rocked back and forth, holding my knee in my hands. "This is so *stupid!*" I shouted at the empty room. "What am I *doing* here? Who ever heard of the greatest treasure in the world being in a *church?*"

I was angrier than ever now . . . and more determined than ever to get at that light. I stood slowly to my feet and limped towards the light—being careful not to run into any more pews.

As I came nearer, I began to think that this was no ordinary light. Most sources of light give off light to other things around it—like a nightlight in a dark hallway or a flashlight in a dark room. This source of light lit up itself and nothing else so that it appeared to be suspended in midair.

What *was* it? It was too small to be a cracked doorway and too large to be a candle. And it didn't possess the shape of either.

Then I recognized it. *"The key!"*

At that moment, I didn't wonder how the key had gotten into the room. Nor did I wonder why the key was glowing in the dark like a glow-in-the-dark sticker. All I could think about was the fact that I had finally found it and that this key would lead me to the treasure.

The key wasn't in a flat position like you would expect a key to look that was resting on a table or a desk. It was upright and the front part of it was missing—as if it were already inside a lock.

"Maybe this is the door that will lead me to the treasure!" I thought out loud. And with this in mind, I reached for the key and turned it.

CHAPTER 10

The Mission

I found myself on the floor again with another sharp pain—this time in my head.

What had just happened? It had happened so fast, I wasn't sure. I thought I remembered seeing a flash of light for a split-second, right after I had turned the key. But I couldn't be sure.

I rubbed the back of my head. It was throbbing. What had I hit my head on? I turned around: a wooden pew was directly behind me.

"Another pew," I moaned, still rubbing my head. "I hate churches."

I started trying to get up. I was almost to my feet when a powerful force hit me in the side of the head. Instinctively, I dropped to the floor.

I looked up. I didn't believe what I saw: about three feet directly above my head was a steady stream of light piercing the darkness—wide and straight and almost dancing. I had never before seen a light like this. It almost seemed to be alive. It was rectangular in shape—resembling a horizontal searchlight.

I was in awe. I sat there with my mouth open for probably a minute. Then I slowly and carefully (I did *not* want to get hit in the head again) crawled out from under the light and stood up. I saw where the light was coming from: where the golden key had been was a book—propped open and resting on some kind of table but, like with the key, it illuminated only itself so I couldn't tell what it was actually sitting on. Once again, it appeared to be floating in midair. The beam of light was being emitted from this book.

I stood there in silence, as though I were in the presence of something holy and great. Then I began to walk towards it. I turned my head once (but only once) to see how far the light stretched out behind me. The golden beam reached all the way to the very back of the sanctuary.

When I was only a foot away from the book, I automatically reached out my hand to touch it, then hesitated. What if I received some kind of electric shock? I hadn't yet forgotten the blow I had received to my head. Slowly and cautiously, I reached my hand into the stream of light: It swept my hand back as if the light were a raging river surging through the center of the room. The mere force of it nearly knocked me over.

Now I was enchanted. This was the most awesome phenomenon I had ever seen.

"Cool!" I exclaimed.

I began thinking of all the possibilities. I could take the book back to my hometown and show it to all my friends. I would be the most popular kid in school! People would come to interview me and write articles about me—I would be famous! And if someone was bothering me, all I'd have to do was to pull out this book, open it up, and knock them over with its light! "Like a giant light saver!" I thought out loud. Risa was right: This *was* the greatest treasure in the world!

I reached out to take the book.

"The book has been utilized as a weapon many a time,"

came a voice. "You would not be the first."

I spun around. Sitting in the front pew—where just a moment ago I had bumped my head—was the man with wings I had met in Paraíso. Only now, the enormous wings were missing, along with his sword. Otherwise he looked exactly as I remembered him: kind, white-robed, strong, terrifying.

I stood there petrified as the giant man (appearing *much* more intimidating on Earth than he had in Paraíso) stood up from the pew, walked over to the open book (he walked right through the light without any trouble at all!), picked it up, and closed it. The moment the book closed, the flow of light was cut off—a little bit at a time, like light shining through a closing door. When the book closed, the room became completely dark (except for the light that seemed to linger around the giant man like a halo).

He was now sitting on the pew again. "Come," he said with a smile, indicating with a pat that the space to his right was available.

I slowly made my way over to the pew and sat down next to him. I knew he could be trusted—I'd seen evidence of his kindness—and yet I *still* couldn't get over my fear of him. He looked so incredibly powerful.

He seemed to understand. "I see you have discovered the Book of Light, little one," he said, smiling down at me. "This is good. It will aid you on your quest."

My quest? I had thought that discovering the book *was* my quest.

"Do you remember my name?" he asked, smiling.

I shook my head.

"Mensajero, and yours is Sara, correct?"

I nodded.

"Do you remember my occupation, Sara?"

I stopped to think. Even if I *did* manage to remember, would I be able to get the words out? Somehow I managed.

"You—you," I stuttered in a feeble voice I didn't know I possessed, "you deliver messages?"

His bright face lit up even more. "Yes!" he exclaimed. (His enormous wings most likely would have been flapping right now had he had them.) "You remember well, little one," Mensajero grinned. "And that is why I am here at this time—to deliver to you a message from the King." He paused, his face becoming graver. He seemed hesitant to give me the message. "He has sent me to inform you," he said bleakly, "that your father is in great jeopardy."

Great jeopardy. Did that mean that my dad was in trouble?

"He needs your help, Sara," he said.

Suddenly, I had a flashback as my mother's words were recalled to my mind: *"Take care of your Dad, will you, Sara?"* she had said to me. *"He will need your help."*

For a minute I was speechless. Mensajero gave me all the time I needed to gather my thoughts. "What does he need help with?" I asked faintly.

The compassionate man looked away, a look of deep sorrow in his crystal blue eyes. It seemed that his job of delivering messages was not a pleasant one for him today. "Your father has been hurt, Sara," he said in a hushed tone. "Those who have been hurt need help the most."

I was starting to feel worried. "My dad's been hurt?"

Mensajero turned to me, looking me directly in the eyes and taking my hands in his. "Yes, little one," he said, "but not in the way you think. He has not been hurt physically but in other ways. Only the King can heal him, but you can help, Sara. You can be a listening ear. Sometimes that is all that is needed."

I sat there in silence. I didn't know what to say.

Mensajero lifted the book from his lap and placed it in my hands. "The Book of Light is a powerful weapon," he said to me, "—sharper than any two-edged sword. Use it well. It was written by none other than the King of Paraíso himself (blessed be his name forever and ever!), and reading it will reveal much. Ask Espíritu for guidance in its use—as it is his to use as he pleases. Listen to Espíritu, Sara, and you will grow wise."

Mensajero rose suddenly to his feet. "I must leave you now," he said. "My mission here on Earth is complete— the King is calling me home. Fulfill *your* mission, Sara." And with that, he vanished, leaving me to stare into utter darkness.

CHAPTER 11

The Book of Light

I sat there in the darkness, blinking my eyes and wondering whether I had really just spoken with Mensajero or if the whole thing had been a side effect from the bump on my head. Then I felt the Book of Light in my hands. Yes, it had really happened.

I couldn't decide if I was happy about this or not. As exciting as it can be to get a personal message delivered to you by a criado (was that what the guys were called?), the message was hardly a pleasant one. If it had really happened, then that meant that my dad really did need my help.

With this realization, I stood quickly to my feet. My dad was hurt; I had to get home as soon as possible. Unfortunately, I overlooked the fact that I was presently in a dark room and would be best advised to walk slowly. I found myself on the floor again with another bruised knee beside another wooden pew. I would definitely be limping home today.

"Where is that book?" I demanded.

I felt around on the floor for it. When I'd found it, I pulled it over to myself and opened it up. This was mistake number two. The light that entered my eyes was no ordinary light: it stung like salt water and burned like fire. The pain was so bad that I forgot all about the pain in my knee. I cried out in agony—slamming the book shut as fast as I could and throwing it halfway across the room. After the several minutes it took me to recover (I was still seeing spots, however), I began feeling around on the floor for it again. I was determined to get out of this place without hitting any more pews, and I would need that blasted book to help me.

It took me a long time of crawling around on the floor to finally find it, but find it I did. I took the book in my hands and—careful this time to point the book *away* from my face—opened it up. The light shot out of it like a laser beam—illuminating as bright as day everything in its path. This book would help me to find my way home.

I pointed the book at the floor and began walking. It did me no good to aim it at the back of the room (which was, of course, my destination) because, as I mentioned previously, the book lit up only those things which were directly in its path. Aiming the light towards the back of the room would light up the back of the room very nicely, but the space immediately in front of me would still be covered in total darkness. So I pointed the light at my feet and allowed the book to light my path.

With the help of the book, I made my way safely out of the sanctuary, down the hall, and out the eastern door. Once outside, I closed the book and stuck it under my arm. I looked at the sky: it was a lot later than I thought. Then it occurred to me: I had been gone all day without telling anybody where I was going (of course, at the time, I hadn't even known myself). Boy, was I going to get it when I got home. I began walking briskly in the direction of Uncle Antonio's house.

I wasn't afraid of getting lost; I knew this town well— even in the dark. This town, you may recall, had been my

yearly summer vacation spot for many years. I could probably find my way back with my eyes closed. I knew where I
was because I recognized this church (as I pointed out
earlier) as being the church that we always drove by on our
way out of town. There was a large city to the east of us that
we enjoyed visiting because it had a large mall where we
could spend all day shopping (one of Aunt Sarah's favorite
things to do) and not come home till late. Always I would
see this church on our way back into town; it was my first
indication that we were nearly home.

Thankfully, I'd always been good with directions. I
knew that—if the city was located to the *east* of us—getting
home required me to go *west*. I also knew another helpful
bit of information (which, if you don't already know, I
suggest you learn) that the sun always sets in the west.
Therefore, I had but to look at the sky, see which way the
sun was setting, and walk that way.

The most beautiful thing in the world after a sunrise
(and, of course, a white horse) is a sunset. Like in a sunrise,
the first color you see in a sunset is pink. After that it's
mostly green and purple. Sometimes there will happen to be
clouds on the western horizon that seem to take on the
appearance of stair steps—leading up to some mysterious
place in the sky. That's what I was gazing at now: pink stair-
step clouds.

"It's not all that mysterious," I thought aloud. "I've been
there before."

The church was located not far from the farm, so it
didn't take me long to reach the long, dusty dirt road that led
up to Uncle's Antonio's farm. Only a few short hours ago, I
thought with a smile, I had crossed this road by way of a
white horse with wings.

As I neared the house, I noticed that a light was on in
one of the windows. "Oh, great," I said to myself. "If Dad's
waiting up for me, he's not going to be in a good mood."

But when I opened the front door and stepped inside, no one was there. "He probably got tired of waiting up for me and went to bed," I sighed. "Now I'm going to be in even *more* trouble!"

I quickly changed clothes, set the book on Jaime's desk, and then slipped as quietly as possible into the bottom bunk. I hoped Jaime was already asleep. No such luck.

"Where've you been?" came a voice from above me.

"None of your business," I retorted.

"Hey, guess what?" Jaime continued, despite my obvious lack of geniality. "My parents are taking us to the lake tomorrow!"

"That's great, now go to sleep, Jaime."

"And do you know what else?" came the voice from above my head.

"I mean it, Jaime."

"I can show you my new secret hiding place that I found there! It's *really* cool! You can hide there *forever* and no one would ever find you!"

I think I'll leave you there, I thought. "I'm going to sleep now, Jaime. Good night."

"And do you know what else?"

"Jaime?"

"What?"

"Good night."

CHAPTER 12

The Decision

I awoke the next morning to a bright light shining in my face. I groaned and rolled over to face the other direction. I was half asleep and half awake when I started wondering what the bright light had been.

I sat straight up in bed. Sunlight from Jaime's window was filling the room.

I sighed and laid back down. "I thought Jaime might have found the book," I said to myself.

The book. Where was it? Was it still on his desk?

I jumped up and ran over to the desk. The book was still there.

Again, I breathed a sigh of relief. *If Jaime ever finds out about this book*, I thought to myself, *the world will never hear the end of it.*

I stood there looking down at it. Did the book hold the same magic now that it did last night?

I looked back at the beds. The top bunk was empty. Today was Sunday—Jaime had gone to church with his family. He would be gone for a while.

I looked back down at the book. Just barely legible on

the cover were the words "The Book of Light."

Just look at it! I thought to myself. *It's so old!* I picked it up—being careful not to open it. *See? See how the cover is falling apart? See how the pages are worn and faded? Surely nothing worthwhile can come from a book such as this.*

The longer I held it, though, the stronger the desire became to open it, so I dropped it back onto the desk.

It would be a waste of time, I continued in the conversation with myself. *I have better things to do than to go through a ratty old book.*

But since nothing came to mind, I sat down at the desk. For some reason, as soon as I sat down, I began to feel sleepy.

It's Sunday, I thought to myself. *I should be in bed.*

I placed my hand on the book's cover. I tried to open the book, but my hand wouldn't cooperate.

What would Jaime think, the voice in my head continued, *if he walked in and saw me sitting here reading a dusty old book?*

I considered the question. I decided I didn't give a hoot what Jaime thought and opened the book.

Light came pouring out—hitting me in the face like a giant wind and nearly knocking me over—piercing my eyes like a thousand needles. I screamed and shoved the book away from me as hard as I could. By the time I was able to see properly again, several minutes had past.

I was mad now. I was going to read that stupid book if it killed me. I looked down at it from a safe distance away. "I can read it without being in the light," I announced triumphantly to no one in particular.

For some reason (I guess I'd read too many *other* stories about magic books), I thought that the book would be difficult to read—written in some foreign language or some mysterious incantation that I wouldn't be able to understand. So when I discovered that it was written in plain

English, I was a little disappointed. Now I had no more excuses not to read it.

So I started reading:

"Espíritu gives life; the flesh counts for nothing. The words I have spoken to you are spirit and they are life."

"This book *is* hard to read!" I corrected myself.

Confident now that I would get nothing out of it anyway, I reached into the light (it wasn't easy—like experiencing a torrent of water pushing against your arm) and turned a few pages over. I looked down at the page:

"For the King so loved the world that he gave his one and only Son, that whoever believes in him shall not perish but have eternal life."

I sat there for a moment in silence. This passage was not as hard to understand. I read it through again. "I wonder if that's what Risa meant," I thought aloud, "when she said that you could 'guarantee your place' in Paraíso by believing in the King's son."

I read on:

"For the King did not send his Son into the world to condemn the world, but to save the world through him. Whoever believes in him is not condemned, but whoever does not believe stands condemned already because he has not believed in the name of the King's one and only Son. This is the verdict: Light has come into the world, but men loved darkness instead of light because their deeds were evil. Everyone who does evil hates the light, and will not come into the light for fear that his deeds will be exposed. But whoever lives by the truth comes into the light, so that it may be seen plainly that what he has done has been done through the King."

I stopped reading. I didn't really understand what I had just read, but I felt as though it held some kind of great significance. "'Whoever lives by the truth comes into the light,'" I repeated aloud.

Just then, I heard my name being called from down the hall. I slammed the book shut just in time to see Jaime come bursting through the door.

"C'mon, Sara," he said, grinning from ear to ear. "Hurry up and get your swimsuit on! We're fixing to leave for the lake!"

"All right, all right," I said. "I'm comin'."

The door slammed closed.

I went and found my swimsuit and quickly put it on. Then I went and jumped into Uncle Antonio's and Aunt Sarah's Suburban and we headed for the lake. Dad was still in bed so he didn't go.

The trip to the lake didn't take very long—only about four or five minutes. Today it seemed a lot longer, though. I couldn't stop thinking about what I had read in the Book of Light: *"Whoever lives by the truth comes into the light"* and *"whoever believes in him shall not perish but have eternal life."* What did it all mean?

Does it mean, I wondered as we drove along, *that if I believe in the King's son, I will get to go live in Paraíso some day? Is that what Risa said? She said that all I had to do was follow the King and believe in the Prince. Was she serious? Is that all I have to do?* It almost seemed too easy.

I had so many questions, and I wished someone were there to answer them for me. I was surprised to find myself actually wishing that I had the Book of Light with me at that moment so that I could try to look up the answers.

Risa had said that the King of Paraíso was also the King of my world. Did that mean that he knew what was happening down here on Earth? If so, did that mean that he knew what was going on with me right now? Was he watching me? Could he *hear* me?

Dear King, I said in my mind, unsure of how to address a king, *if you can hear me right now, and if you even care about what's going on in my life, I just want you to know that I read your book today. It said that in order to go live with you in Paraíso some day I needed to believe in your son, the Prince. I do believe in him, King of Paraíso. Save me and help me to want to follow you. Doing things my way never has worked. Help me learn how to do things your way. Change my heart and give me the courage and strength I need to come into the light. If coming into the light means reading your book and doing what it says, I'll try.*

I sat there waiting for something magical to happen, but nothing happened. "I guess that's the end of that," I said to myself.

Little did I know it was just the beginning.

CHAPTER 13

The Belt of Truth

When we arrived at the lake, Aunt Sarah barked out all of her instructions. (Actually, it was more of a whimper than a bark because of that nicey-nice voice of hers.) She told Jaime not to go too far out into the water and me to keep an eye on him and both of us not to wander off too far because lunch would be ready soon. After agreeing to all of her conditions, Jaime and I left the Suburban and headed for the water.

The lake was not very large, but big enough to take a boat out on it. I'd seen boats on it before and always wished that Uncle Antonio and Aunt Sarah had one. They had enough money for a boat, so why didn't they just go ahead and buy one?

Jaime was already halfway to the water by now. Uncle Antonio and Aunt Sarah began taking sacks out of the back of the Suburban. There was a grill nearby, and Uncle Antonio was going to grill hamburgers. I preferred hot dogs, but I didn't complain.

"C'mon!" Jaime said, running back to take me by the hand. I jerked my hand away and he ran on without me. I didn't care if I was being a pain. I didn't really even want to be here in the first place; I preferred to be back home in bed.

As Jaime neared the water, he ran behind a small hill and disappeared. For a moment, I wondered what had happened to him. Then, as I got closer, I noticed that the hill—into which a small pier had been built for boat loading—was slightly eroded, and therefore a kind of cave had formed. Jaime was inside the "cave."

"Come on in, Sara!" he called to me from inside the cave.

Great, I thought with disgust. *It's probably nice and muddy in there.* The indention was not a large one, so I had to bend down in order to walk inside. It was true I liked secret places, but this was *not* my idea of a good time.

"Isn't this great?" Jaime exclaimed, crouching on the ground. "It's like a cave, isn't it?"

"It's dark and gloomy in here," I complained.

"Then you should like it just fine!" Jaime laughed.

"That's it, I'm leaving."

"Wait! Don't you want to pretend like we're explorers discovering this cave for the first time?"

"I think I'll go explore out here for a while," I said, and quickly made my escape before Jaime could make any more objections.

I walked over to the water, prepared to wash off. But I really hadn't gotten all that muddy so I headed on up the hill to the pier. I could sit up here for a while and get some sun. If I couldn't be at home sleeping, at least I could use this day to work on my tan.

The wooden pier felt warm beneath my feet. I walked over to the edge, sat down, and dangled my legs off the end of the pier. The pier hung out over the water far enough and was far enough above the water's surface that I didn't worry about Jaime coming along and trying to pull me in. Besides, if he tried it I would kick him in the teeth.

It was so quiet here—so peaceful. *If only I were completely alone right now,* I thought to myself, *I know I would be completely happy.*

I looked out over the water. Sunlight glimmered on the water's surface. A couple of waterfowl flew in—skimming across the surface and settling onto the lake. I caught sight of a fish jump not too far away. Apart from all human interaction (especially Jaime), I found that I could enjoy myself.

The sky was even more beautiful than the lake. The sun was peeking through the clouds causing there to be an outburst of light so that the sun's rays shot out in all directions. I recognized one of the clouds to be a thunderhead—the kind of cloud that is incredibly tall and beautifully white but always brings rain. My mother used to say, "A gorgeous sky in the afternoon means a stormy sky at night," and she was nearly always right. It would rain tonight. But that was okay with me; I *loved* the rain—*especially* at night. I loved listening to it while lying in bed—the rhythmic tapping lulling me to sleep. And in the morning there would be that sweet after-the-rain scent still lingering in the air.

I had sat there enjoying the tranquility for no time at all when I heard someone calling my name. It was Aunt Sarah telling Jaime and me that lunch was ready.

Begrudgingly, I stood to my feet. I watched as Jaime ran out from under the pier below me and started towards the picnic area. He looked pretty muddy; Aunt Sarah would make him wash up before lunch.

I was about to turn around and head back when I happened to look down at my reflection. Jaime had stepped into the lake just moments before on his way out of the cave, so there were still ripples moving through the water. I couldn't see my reflection clearly, but something about it bothered me; something didn't look quite right.

As the ripples subsided, I studied my reflection in the water below. It looked as though some metal object were wrapped around my waist.

I looked down at my own waist; nothing was there.

I looked at my reflection again. The lake was nearly placid now so that my reflection could be seen as clearly as if I were looking into a mirror. I appeared to be wearing a belt of some kind—a very wide, very shiny silver belt. Light from the sun was reflecting off of it.

Could it be something *beneath* the surface of the water that I was seeing—like a tin can or a soda can? This was a lake, after all: one oftentimes sees trash in a lake due to the lack of consideration given by careless lake-goers. It didn't look much like a tin can or a soda can, though; it was much too large.

I put my hands on my hips. In real life I was touching my swimsuit; in my reflection I was touching a large metal belt. It was much wider than a normal belt—overlapping quite a bit of my swimsuit. And it looked as though (if I could actually feel it on me) it would be quite heavy since it appeared to be made entirely out of metal.

What was going on here?

"Sara, lunch is ready," I heard Aunt Sarah call to me from the picnic area.

Oh, well, I would have to worry about this some other time. I turned and headed down the hill and over to the picnic area where Jaime, Uncle Antonio, and Aunt Sarah were waiting.

CHAPTER 14

The Storm

I couldn't even enjoy the rest of my afternoon at the lake for worrying about what I had seen in the water. As I have mentioned before, I'm the kind of person who has to understand things, or else I go crazy. *What was that thing around my waist in my reflection, and why couldn't I see it in real life?*

Could it have been my imagination? Could I have just *thought* I saw something when really there was nothing there at all? Maybe. But it wasn't like me to imagine things. And it had looked much too real to be imagined anyway.

I decided that when I got back to the house I would look again; I would look in the mirror and there would be nothing there. I would discover that the silver belt had in fact been a figment of my imagination, probably brought on by too much time spent in the sun—or a lack of sleep.

But when our day at the lake was finished and we headed for home and I ran into the house—heading straight for the bathroom and locking the door behind me—I discovered in amazement that the silver belt was still there.

I put my hands on my hips, standing opposite the bath-room mirror. Again, my hands appeared to be resting on a thick metal belt, and again they touched nothing but my swimsuit. The belt was about a foot in width and looked to be at least a couple inches thick. I also noticed something else I hadn't noticed before: a long, silver sheath (the place where a sword is kept) was attached to the belt on the left-hand side. It looked similar to the one I remembered Mensajero wearing except that this one was silver instead of gold, and of course it wasn't nearly as large. This one was also different from his in that it was empty; there was no sword inside.

This was the most bizarre thing that had ever happened to me. I thought about what to do. Should I tell someone? No, they would probably just think I was crazy. (Aunt Sarah would probably make me go to the doctor.) Should I worry about it hurting me? Was I carrying around some kind of invisible metal belt (that, for some reason, was only visible in reflections) that was a part of some kind of conspiracy in which someone was trying to track me—recording every-thing I did and said?

I leaned up closer to the mirror. There appeared to be a symbol in the center of the belt's buckle. I moved around a bit so that the light would catch it at just the right angle. It was the letter "T."

I tried to imagine what the "T" might stand for: Terrorist? Tyrant? Technological Tracking?

Well, there was one "T" word that it was definitely beginning to stand for: Tired. I quickly changed into my regular clothes, hung my swimsuit in the bathroom to dry, and then hit the bottom bunk for a quick nap.

The nap must have lasted a little longer than I antici-pated because I woke up to darkness and the sound of rolling thunder. What time was it? Had I really slept from 3:00 in the afternoon all the way till nightfall?

The first thing I thought of was that I still hadn't gotten a chance to talk with Dad. *Now he's going to be* really *mad,* I thought dismally.

From far away, I heard the sound of distant thunder. I had learned in my school science class that you can tell how close a storm is by how loud the thunder is. If the thunder is not very loud, then the storm is still quite a ways away. That was the case right now, although it was rapidly getting closer. I smiled; I loved the sound of thunder. My mother had been right once again: a gorgeous sky in the afternoon really *does* mean a stormy sky at night.

As I lay still on the bottom bunk, I could hear Jaime's slow and steady breathing above me. I knew he was sleeping.

I heard another roll of thunder. It was a little louder this time, and I could hear the wind outside the window beginning to blow. Storms had never frightened me; I knew they were just a part of nature, and the only way you could get hurt by one was to be out in the middle of one or—if it were a lightning storm—to be too close to a piece of electronic equipment. I was neither at the moment, so I knew I was safe.

A bolt of lightning lit up the room so brightly and so suddenly that it startled me. It was followed by a crash of thunder that I was afraid might wake up Jaime, but afterwards I could still hear the sound of his relaxed breathing so I knew he was still asleep.

The rain was coming down now in torrents, and the tree right outside Jaime's window had a branch that kept scratching against the house so that it sounded like a person was trying to get in. I knew it was just my imagination, though; I was perfectly safe in here.

The next thunderbolt was louder than before, and this time I really did jump. The lightning that had come before it had lit up the room as bright as day, and even though it had lasted for only a couple seconds it was long enough to reveal what seemed to have been a figure standing over by the bed. I told myself that it was only my imagination—that it had simply been another illusion, like the belt.

I pulled the cover up a little higher around me. My heart was beating faster now. *There is no one in the room, Sara,* I told myself. *You're just imagining things again.*

Lightning struck again. This time I was certain I had seen someone—only five feet from the bed. *Someone was in the room with me!*

My breathing became heavier; I tried holding my breath. I had heard that the best thing to do if there is ever a burglar in the house is not to panic but to ignore him and let him leave; if he gets scared, he might do more damage than he would have done otherwise. I didn't want to scare him.

Then I thought of something: What if it was Mensajero? He had shown up in the dark once before; why couldn't he be doing it again? But if it was Mensajero, then why was he just standing there? Why wasn't he delivering his message?

I debated what to do. I finally decided to risk it. "Mensajero," I whispered as softly as I could manage. "Mensajero, is that you?"

My heart leapt as I saw the dark shadow move. I couldn't see the figure clearly, of course, because it was nearly completely dark in the room.

Suddenly, a bolt of lightning lit up the room—at least, I thought it was a bolt of lightning until the light came and then didn't go away. The light lingered around a tall figure with wings standing directly beside the bed. I couldn't see the figure's face at first because it appeared to be looking up at the ceiling.

Then it looked down at me. Slowly and silently, the figure took a step closer to the bed—kneeling down on one knee. "Hello, Sara," said a strange voice.

CHAPTER 15

Fuego

I looked at the man with wings kneeling beside my bed. Instead of Mensajero's crystal-blue eyes, these eyes were hazel (although they still seemed to shine like Mensajero's). And instead of Mensajero's smooth face, this face was covered by a bushy reddish-brown beard. This criado was similar to Mensajero, however, in that he too looked incredibly strong and carried a sword at his side.

"Hello, Sara," he repeated. His voice was gruff and deep. "The King said you wanted to talk with me. So . . . what do you want?"

I looked at him. What did I want? I just wanted to know who it was that was standing by my bed in the middle of the night, that's all.

"Well?" he said impatiently as I said nothing. "Come on, I have a job to do. Tell me what you wanted to say." The criado looked suddenly up at the ceiling, his face turning very white. "I'm sorry," he apologized quickly.

Was he apologizing to me? I didn't think so.

He looked down at me again. "I guess we can't really talk in here," he said in a meeker tone. "Come on, let's go into another room." He stood quickly to his feet and walked over to the door. "You coming?" he said, turning to look at me.

I didn't see as though I had much of a choice, so I got out of bed and followed the criado (who was not as tall as Mensajero—closer to seven feet instead of nine—but still no midget) out of Jaime's bedroom. I looked behind me; amazingly, Jaime had slept through the criado's loud talking. As I followed the winged man into the kitchen, I found myself glad that I had fallen asleep wearing a t-shirt and shorts instead of my nightclothes.

The criado turned on the kitchen light (I didn't see him flip a switch, but he must have because the light came on) and took a seat on one of the bar stools. I hoped it would hold him. I nervously sat down beside him.

"So . . ." he said, looking at me disinterestedly. "Is this your house?"

I sat there for a minute, unsure of how to answer him. He sighed impatiently at my hesitation and propped his head up on the bar with his arm. "I—I don't live here normally," I stuttered, looking up at him. "Only during the summer." I knew this answer was inadequate, but I was too nervous to know exactly what to say.

He sat there waiting for me to continue, and when I didn't he put his arm down—nodding his head rapidly and sighing heavily. "Well, I'll be very honest with you, Sara," he said, looking at me. "Most of my jobs as guardian involve adults. The last three were all adults. I don't like working with kids, understand? No offense, but I just don't like it."

What was I supposed to say? I felt uncomfortable enough already talking to a seven-foot guy with wings and a sword. But to have one tell you that he didn't like "working with" you was a thousand times worse.

"But now that I'm here," he continued, apparently not wanting to hurt my feelings *too* badly, "I wouldn't mind a glass of wine."

I looked up at him, surprised.

"Just a taste," he reassured me. "I don't have a problem with self-control."

"I—I don't think we have any," I told him. As a matter of fact, I *knew* we didn't have any; Uncle Antonio and Aunt Sarah didn't drink, and they had strict rules about keeping any kind of alcoholic beverage in the house.

"You sure about that?" the criado asked me, raising his eyebrows. He nodded toward the refrigerator. "Go check it out."

I got up and walked over to the refrigerator, opening the door. Sure enough, a bottle of wine was sitting there on the top shelf.

"Bring two glasses," the criado said.

I had mixed feelings at this point. I had never tasted wine before because I had never been allowed to; Dad said I was too young. Still, I did wonder what it tasted like. By the time I had returned with two small glasses, I had made up my mind that it wouldn't be such a terrible thing for me to have just a sip. (After all, it was being recommended by the highest authority!) But as the criado opened up the bottle and poured the red liquid into my glass, I noticed that it tasted very much like red Kool-Aid.

"Is this wine?" I asked him.

He finished off the small amount of wine he had poured for himself before answering. "Sure it is," he said, setting his glass down with a clank. But I noticed that he gave me a quick wink, and there was a smile hidden beneath his beard.

I couldn't get over how different this criado was from Mensajero. Mensajero had used fancy speech in his conversations; this criado talked like a regular person. Mensajero had been so proper; this criado was much more casual. Mensajero had been so nice and friendly; this criado was a grouch. I liked this criado.

"I guess the polite thing to do would be to introduce

myself," the criado said, pouring a bit more wine into his glass. "I have another name, but the name I most often go by is Fuego." He chuckled to himself. "I guess my nickname fits me pretty well," he said.

"It's nice to meet you," I said, slowly extending my hand.

He looked down at it, then up at me. I saw him smile, and he released his glass—taking my hand in his own and engaging me in a vigorous handshake that nearly knocked me off my stool. "Nice to meet you, Sara!" he said in a booming voice. "I'm sorry for coming across as such a grump. I admit that when I found out yesterday that I was going to be assigned to a child, I was less than thrilled about it. But I can see now that you are no ordinary child. You are a very polite young lady."

I blushed.

"And please don't think that I'm a typical criado," he continued. "Most are more like Mensajero—just as sweet as they can be from the tops of their heads to the tips of their snow-white wings. I just never adopted that personality style."

I smiled. "Me neither," I said quietly. I thought for a moment. "And—and that's okay," I continued as Fuego went back to his drink. "Everybody's different. I thought that Mensajero was too nice, anyway."

Fuego choked on his drink and nearly sent wine spewing all over the kitchen. (What a mess *that* would have been!) "You've met Mensajero?" he bellowed after he'd recovered. "Where?"

His reaction had surprised me, so it took me a few seconds to answer him. "The—the first time was in Paraíso—"

"You've met with him more than once?" he interrupted, even louder than before.

I nodded timidly. "Yes," I answered him. "The other time was in a church—"

"In a *church?*" (I hoped he wouldn't wake anybody up with all his shouting.) "He came to the *Earth* to meet with you?"

This time it was my turn to sigh and nod; I was tired of being interrupted.

A strange look came into his eyes. He smiled knowingly—looking off into the distance, taking his drink in his hand. "My job may be more interesting than I thought," he said to himself.

I was about to say, "What do you mean?" when I noticed that his gaze had changed. He seemed to be staring hard at something in the living room. The look in his eyes was one of anger mixed with annoyance.

"What is it?" I asked him, following his gaze. The living room was dark and empty, from what I could see.

Fuego didn't respond. Instead, he slammed his glass down on the bar and jumped up from his stool—knocking it over onto the tile floor with a crash. He instantaneously reached for his sword with his right hand, unsheathing it with the sound of scraping metal. Eyes aflame, he started for the living room. In only three strides he was standing in the middle of the dark room.

CHAPTER 16

The Sombra

"Get out, Engaño," I heard him say. Who was Fuego talking to? I didn't see anyone.

After a pause he continued. "Not anymore; you lost that right yesterday, remember? She's a member of the King's family now."

I looked hard into the darkness; I even squinted in an attempt to see better. It was no use—I saw nothing.

"Need I remind you," Fuego continued in his conversation with the invisible being, "that messing with her means messing with the King? I suggest that you leave right now."

Maybe it was just too dark. I hopped down off my stool and walked over to where the living room light was—flipping it on.

"Sara, get back!" Fuego shouted at me, not turning his head.

I stumbled backwards, retreating into the kitchen.

"Is that so?" Fuego continued after another pause. "Well then, why don't you go ahead and try it? What are you waiting for?"

I looked again. Even with the light on I felt just as blind

as before; no one was there except for Fuego. It was like listening to only one side of a telephone conversation.

"The choice is yours, Engaño," Fuego said curtly. "Either flee or fight."

Fuego stood there for about a minute longer. Then he did an about-face and started back towards the kitchen. He picked up the stool he'd knocked over and set it down onto the floor with a bang. He was obviously still upset.

"Who *was* that?" I asked him after he'd had a chance to cool down a bit (and pour himself another glass).

Fuego took a few moments to respond. "Someone who knew better," he finally responded, the sound of anger still apparent in his voice.

"Was it another criado?" I wondered.

Fuego froze—turning to look at me with his glass halfway to his mouth. Very slowly, he set the glass back down onto the bar. He sighed deeply then, looking down at his glass rather than at me, said, "No, Sara. It wasn't a criado . . . not recently, anyway." He had said these last few words more softly than the rest. I didn't know what he meant by this, but I didn't ask.

He paused again—nervously rubbing his thumb along the side of the glass. He seemed to be troubled by what he was about to tell me.

Finally, he looked at me. "It was a sombra, Sara," he said.

Suddenly, I had a flashback; I remembered what Risa had told me in Paraíso: "Now that you have been to Paraíso," I remembered her saying, "you will begin to see things from Paraíso's point of view. You will be able to see both the criados and the sombras for the first time ever."

Fuego noticed me thinking and sat there in silence. "What were you thinking about?" he asked me, seeing that I was finished.

"I was remembering something that someone had told me in Paraíso," I told him. "She had told me that now that I had the Power of Paraíso, I would begin to see things from Paraíso's point of view—and that would mean being able to see both criados and sombras for the first time."

Fuego thought for a moment. "And yet you were not able to see Engaño?" he asked.

I shook my head.

Fuego thought about this, then nodded. "It's just as well," he said.

"Will I ever be able to see him?" I asked.

"I don't know, Sara," Fuego replied. "Only the King knows the answer to that. But I do know this: You must prepare yourself for that day. Sombras aren't like criados, Sara. They're dangerous. They're miserable creatures— former criados who chose to turn against the King. Now they no longer serve the King but fight *against* him. It is the responsibility of both the criados (those who remained faithful to the King, that is) and the warriors to fight against the sombras. But, of course, neither the criados nor the warriors are able to do this without the King's help."

"Who are the warriors?" I asked.

"Well . . . you, for one," Fuego smiled. "Any human that has chosen to join with the criados in serving the King is a warrior."

I smiled. I liked the idea of being considered a "warrior."

"But *never*—under *any* circumstances, Sara—try to fight a sombra by your own power," Fuego warned. "Many a warrior has tried this and failed. You must rely on the King's power to defeat them."

"How do I get the King's power?" I inquired.

Fuego grinned and I saw his wings begin to move. *Oh, great.* I thought. *He really is going to knock me off the stool this time!* But, thankfully, the criado was able to control himself and presently stilled his wings. "The King's power, Sara," Fuego responded, "is obtained through personal communication with the King himself—when you talk to him and allow him to talk to you. Criados have the privilege of speaking with the King in person. Humans, on the other hand, do not have this privilege . . . not yet, anyway. For now they must rely on other means. The King has written a Book for them—for *you*, Sara—so that you could get to know him on a personal basis. It's called the Book of Light. Have you heard of this Book?"

"It's sitting in there on Jaime's desk," I responded.

"Oh," Fuego said, a little taken aback. "Great. I don't know who Jaime is, but that's not important right now. The important thing is that you've got the Book."

"What's so important about the book?" I questioned.

Again, the criado seemed taken aback. "Have you read it?" he asked.

"A little bit," I answered.

"What did you think of it?"

"It—it was hard to understand," I admitted. "I couldn't make anything of it."

Fuego considered this. "Yes," he said, "I suppose it *would* be hard to understand for a human new to the ways of the King. But it's necessary, Sara. It's one of the clearest and best ways for a warrior to hear the King's voice. It's also one of the most efficient weapons a warrior has against Mentiroso."

"Mentiroso? Who's that?" I asked. "Is he anything like Mensajero?" Their names sure sounded similar.

"Oh, Sara," Fuego sighed, shaking his head, "there never were two more different individuals. They're like night and day. You've met Mensajero, apparently, so you know what he's like. Imagine, if you can, a criado who is the exact *opposite* of Mensajero—as frightening as he is friendly, as cruel as he is kind—and you'll have a pretty clear picture of what Mentiroso is like."

I tried to imagine it. It wasn't a pretty picture.

"Mentiroso is the leader of the sombras," he told me,

"and he does his job well, Sara. Like any effective leader, he is very familiar with the enemy. In fact, I would venture to say, Sara, that Mentiroso is more familiar with the Book of Light than any of the criados—*including* Mensajero.

"But his power does not exceed that of the King," Fuego continued. "This is a *very* important point to remember, Sara. No matter what the danger, always remember that the King is in control. You are his daughter now, and Mentiroso cannot touch you."

Just then, I heard a door open. It had been so quiet up till now (except for the rhythmic pounding of the rain) that the sound made me jump. I looked out the window: the sun was coming up. *That must be Uncle Antonio getting up to feed the horses,* I thought. I wished I could get back to Jaime's room without his seeing me. But this was impossible seeing as how Jaime's room was located at the very end of the hallway.

I turned back to Fuego. The criado was no longer sitting on his stool but rather was standing directly behind me in military position—left hand on his sword, eyes staring straight ahead. I also noticed that the halo of light that had been aglow around him had disappeared. He was back to his job as guardian; our time of conversing was over.

I peered down the dark hallway. I tried to think of some legitimate excuse for me to be sitting in the kitchen at the crack of dawn.

I heard someone cough. A figure slowly emerged out of the darkness—shielding his eyes from the light. "Sara?" said a gruff voice.

It was Dad.

CHAPTER 17

Dad

"Hi, Dad."

At first he didn't say anything, but stood there looking at me strangely, blinking in the light. "Sara?" he repeated.

"Yeah, Dad," I said a little louder, but still softly. For some reason, I always used a softer voice around my dad—I don't know why. "It's me."

"What are you doing up so early?" he asked in his usual gruff voice.

He stumbled into the kitchen and began preparing his typical cup of coffee. I knew that if I waited long enough, I wouldn't have to respond to his question. Most of the time he didn't really want to talk anyway.

I was right. He started fixing his coffee and forgot all about me.

I suddenly thought of the wine; Dad would kill me if he saw it sitting there. I looked down at the bar but it was gone. I looked behind me at Fuego; he must have disposed of it. Then I began to wonder if my dad was able to see the man with wings standing directly behind me. Dad turned around to face me. Apparently not, I decided. Either that or my dad was more tired than I thought.

"Where were you Saturday?" he suddenly asked.

"Saturday?" I said. I knew I couldn't play dumb with my dad. But it never hurt to try. "Saturday? Let's see, that was the day before yesterday? I think I was—"

"You were gone all day," he abruptly finished for me. "Where were you?"

One thing about my dad was—if he ever *did* decide to talk—there was no escaping him. "I—I lost track of the time," I said, "and—"

"That's not what I asked," he interrupted me.

I thought about how to best answer him. *Well, let's see. I was several places on Saturday: On a flying horse. In cloudland. In a church.* I decided to go with the latter. "I was in a church," I told him.

Unfortunately, this elicited the same response as had I said "cloudland." "A church?" he said, stopping in the middle of what he was doing to turn and glare at me. "What were you doing in a church?"

It was a natural question—especially for someone like me who hated churches.

What was I supposed to say? I hardly knew the answer myself. I only went in there because Espíritu wanted me to. "I—I'm not sure," I answered truthfully.

"Well, you can be sure of this," he responded quickly and curtly. "You won't be going there again."

This was always how conversations about church went with my dad. For some reason, he possessed an intense dislike for churches, and nothing would ever change his mind.

When I didn't respond (because I knew better than to do so), he scooped up his cup of coffee and headed for the living room—flopping down in his favorite place to sit: Uncle Antonio's easy chair. No sooner had he sat down than he propped up the leg rest, reached for the remote, and turned on the TV. It was like a package deal that always went together.

I sat there for a minute on my stool, looking at him. I looked at Fuego: he looked about the same. I looked back at Dad. All of a sudden, I remembered something that Mensajero had told me: My dad was hurt.

I looked at him. He didn't *look* hurt—he just looked tired. But I decided to walk over and make sure.

I got down off my stool and walked into the living room. (Fuego followed right behind me—just in case that sombra thing came back, I guess.) I took a seat on the couch catty-corner from the easy chair. From here I could see both my dad and—if I turned my head—the TV...not that there was really much to see at this point. The guy was only talking about boring stuff like the weather and the upcoming week's 7-day forecast. It was pointless...not only for me, but for my dad. I knew that if I asked him 5 minutes from now what the weather would *most likely* be this week (weathermen can never *really* know for sure, you know), he wouldn't even have a clue. Like most times, he was watching television solely for the sake of watching television. It was what he did when there was nothing else to do which, for my dad, was most of the time.

"Dad?" I interrupted the weatherman as he spoke of sunny days. "Dad, can I ask you a question?"

He expectantly continued to sit there—eyes glued to the TV set. I would obviously have to try something a little more drastic. "Dad, why don't you like to talk about church?"

This elicited the desired response; at least he took his eyes off the TV. "What?" he said.

"Why—" I looked down, finding it impossible to look at his eyes. "Why don't you like to talk about church?" I repeated meekly.

For a few seconds he said nothing. I continued looking

down—too afraid to make eye contact. Finally, I looked up: his eyes were back on the television set again. He had once again completely avoided the question.

Now normally at this point, I would have given up and probably left the room. I would not have pursued the topic; when my dad stopped talking, so did I. But on this day, I felt different somehow. I felt like I wanted to be answered for once.

"The church was really nice, Dad," I continued quickly, the noise from the TV still in the background. "It had stained-glass windows, big double doors…"

"I *told* you," my dad interrupted abruptly, "we're not *interested* in church."

Maybe you're *not*, I thought to myself. I decided to say it. "Maybe *you're* not," I responded in a quiet voice, continuing to look down, "but *I* am. In fact, it might be nice to visit there some time…"

"Did you hear what I said, Sara?" he responded, his voice rising above that of the weatherman. "Church is not for *us!*"

Normally, I would have shut up at this point and let him win. After all, shouting matches were always about winning, and I could never win in this way against my dad. Besides, arguing is stupid. It's better just to give in and let the other person win.

But not today. "Maybe it's not for *you*," I continued, using my normal tone of voice, "but it might be for *me*. I don't think it would hurt if I just checked it out some time…"

Dad chose this time to check *himself* out. I heard the leg rest from the easy chair fall with a bang, followed by the sound of his feet quickly leaving the room. I heard his coffee cup drop into the sink with a clank and then, moments later, a bedroom door slam behind him.

"Well, that went well," I sighed.

CHAPTER 18

Aunt Sarah

I sat there on the couch for a few minutes, listening to the sound of the rain. It was slowing up now. Soon it would stop altogether. *When will* this *stop?* I asked myself.

I got up from the couch, turned off the TV (Dad had forgotten to), and headed for Jaime's room. I figured Jaime would be up by now. But when I opened the door to his room, I found that the light was still turned off and I could hear the sound of his breathing. *The rain must have kept him asleep,* I thought. *Good. Maybe he'll stay asleep a while longer.*

I looked over at his desk. The Book of Light was resting on top of it. I didn't want to give Jaime the opportunity to find it, so I grabbed it up before leaving.

I walked back to the living room and sat down on the couch again. I considered turning on the TV, but nothing worthwhile would be on at this time anyway. Besides, TVs were starting to annoy me.

I looked down at the book. *I might as well read it,* I thought. *I'm not doing anything else.*

The first thing I did was to tilt the book away from my

face; I was *not* going to allow myself to get blasted like the last few times I'd tried it. Cautiously (and nervously, I might add), I opened the book. Very slowly, I reached my hand into the light. Although the force of the light was still there, I noticed that it didn't seem quite as strong as usual. Either that or *I* was stronger.

Ever so slowly, I tilted the book towards my face. Maybe I would get blasted by the light, maybe I wouldn't, but I felt the need to find out.

The effect of the light on my face was strange. I still felt like it was pushing against me, but—at the same time—I almost felt as though it were pulling me *towards* it, as well. Maybe it was just my imagination. I had been imaging a lot of things lately.

I also noticed that it didn't hurt my eyes as much as it had in the past. The light still stung, but it was bearable now—and it didn't last as long. It was more like the effect of a car's headlights when they hit your eyes: it stings at first, but then it quickly dies away. That's how it was for me now.

I looked down at the passage:

Therefore put on the full armor of the King, so that when the day of evil comes, you may be able to stand your ground, and after you have done everything, to stand. Stand firm then, with the belt of truth buckled around your waist . . .

I stopped reading. "'Belt of truth,'" I said out loud. I suddenly remembered the "T" I had seen on my belt. "Could the 'T' stand for 'truth'?"

I thought about it for a minute, then shrugged and flipped a few pages over. I found something that sounded familiar:

"Espíritu gives life; the flesh counts for nothing. The words I have spoken to you are spirit and they are life."

"What in the world *is* this?" I asked frustratedly. "Who is talking, and what does he mean his words are spirit and life? This book makes absolutely *no* sense whatsoever."

I decided to read the part before to find out which "words" it was talking about. I read the passage aloud:

"I tell you the truth, he who believes has everlasting life. I am the bread of life. Your forefathers ate the manna in the desert, yet they died. But here is the bread that comes down from Paraíso, which a man may eat and not die. I am the living bread that came down from Paraíso. If anyone eats of this bread, he will live forever. This bread is my flesh, which I will give for the life of the world."

I slammed the book shut. "Why do I even bother?" I mumbled. "The book is a bunch of nonsense."

"Sara?"

I spun around. Aunt Sarah was standing near the hallway entrance. She was in her housecoat and her blond hair was pulled up in a clip on top of her head.

I sighed. "I'm sorry, Aunt Sarah. I didn't mean to wake anybody up."

Surprisingly, she didn't answer. Instead, she walked over to where I was and sat down beside me. This bothered me; I scooted over a little.

"You didn't wake me up, Sara," she smiled, putting her arm around me. I scooted away from her a little more. Aunt Sarah took the hint and removed her arm. "I was already up."

I hoped I had offended her but, unfortunately, it didn't appear to have fazed her in the least.

"What's that you're reading?" she asked, pointing to the book.

"Oh, nothing," I sighed. "Nothing important."

"Unless I'm mistaken," she said, "it's *very* important. Isn't that the Book of Light?"

I turned to look at her. "You've seen this book before?" I asked.

"Not only have I seen it," she smiled, her eyes sparkling that annoying sparkle, "I've *read* it!"

"Well," I replied, looking away to avoid her eyes, "it's

pretty boring, if you ask me. It's impossible to understand it."

"Not impossible," she corrected, "just difficult. And I would definitely have to agree with you there."

This surprised me. "If you didn't understand it, then why did you read it?" I asked her.

"Some things come in time," Aunt Sarah replied, "and understanding the Book of Light is one of those things."

"Well, then, do you understand *this* part?" I challenged, flipping through the book. Amazingly, I was somehow able to find the passage I had been reading.

I dropped the Book of Light in her lap and pointed to the passage. Aunt Sarah took a minute to read it. "Yes," she said, handing it back to me, "I can understand why you had trouble understanding that."

"Duh."

"But I can explain it to you, if you like."

"Go ahead," I sighed, slumping down further on the couch. "It's not like there's anything else to do around here."

"Well," she replied, unflustered, "this part is talking about the Prince of Paraíso. Do you know about him?"

I probably knew more than she did. "Yep. You have to believe in him in order to go live in Paraíso," I announced triumphantly.

"Very good," Aunt Sarah nodded. "What does that mean?"

"What does what mean?"

"'Believe in him.' You said that you have to 'believe in' the Prince. What does it mean to believe in him?"

I wasn't expecting to be cross-examined. "*You* know," I said, reaching for an answer, "*believe* in him. Believe that he exists, I guess."

"That's right, Sara," Aunt Sarah responded, "but there's more to it than that. Do you know the rest of it?"

"Aunt Sarah," I sighed, "I'm really no good at guessing games—especially this early in the morning. I'm not a morning person, you know. In fact, maybe I should go back to bed now . . ."

"It also means," she continued, ignoring me completely, "that you have to believe that he died for you—died and rose again. You have to believe that he did this for *you*, Sara, and allow his death to take your place. You have to allow him to be not only the Prince of Paraíso, but also the Prince of your heart and life."

"Right," I said, snapping my fingers. "That's what I meant to say."

"It's the most important decision you'll ever make, Sara," Aunt Sarah said, reaching for my hand. "I hope that you've made it."

"I'm pretty sure I have," I said, jumping off the couch. "Now, if you'll excuse me, Aunt Sarah, I'm going to go back to bed now."

I walked into Jaime's room and tossed the Book of Light onto the desk. I didn't care if I woke Jaime up or not. I flopped down onto the bottom bunk. *That Aunt Sarah*, I thought to myself. *She thinks she knows everything.*

CHAPTER 19

The Breastplate of Righteousness

Over the course of the next few days, I found myself being constantly followed around by a huge guy with wings. Having someone (even a criado) follow you around all the time can get pretty annoying after a while. I wished he would fly away and "protect" someone else—or at least become invisible again. I would have liked a little privacy at times. It's funny, though: He never even *looked* at me! I suppose if you're guarding someone, you can't be looking at the person you're guarding; you have to keep an eye out for the enemy.

I must admit, though, that having my own personal bodyguard made me feel like royalty. "Fuego *did* say that I was the King's daughter now," I boasted to myself, "so that makes me a princess! In a way, I *am* royalty!"

It was obvious that the others couldn't see him. Of course they couldn't. They didn't have the Power of Paraíso like I did.

On Friday, the Power of Paraíso *really* started kicking

in. Aunt Sarah decided to take Jaime and me to the mall. We drove to a nearby city located to the east of us. (Dad didn't go; he stayed back and watched TV. Uncle Antonio stayed with him to keep him company.) Fuego never left my side—even in the Suburban. I could see him outside my window…flying right along beside us.

As soon as we arrived, the three of us (four if you count the criado) walked down past the aisles of cars to the mall entrance. When we got inside, I gasped: there were criados *everywhere!* The big, tall guys with wings and swords were walking alongside many of the shoppers (who were, of course, completely unaware of their presence), causing the place to appear twice as crowded. I wondered for a moment if there would be room enough to walk.

"Wow!" I breathed.

"What is it, Sara?" Aunt Sarah asked, looking at me.

"Oh," I said, feeling my face flush in embarrassment. "I was just noticing: The mall sure is crowded today, isn't it?"

"It sure is," Aunt Sarah nodded. "It usually is on weekends."

She had no idea.

We came to a section of the mall where it was very open—where you could look down from the second floor and see people eating in the food court down below. My breath was taken away at what I saw: Not only people, but winged criados—their wings fully extended, flapping up and down in a steady rhythm as the mighty beings hovered over the oblivious crowd. Near the ceiling were rafters used for holding up the roof; a couple criados could be seen sitting on the rafters!

You cannot imagine (unless you yourself have seen it) what an enormous shock it is to see criados hovering above where you have walked and sitting above where you have sat. Never in my wildest dreams could I have imagined criados looking *this* large and *this* powerful in the air. "If I could do more than just *see* things from Paraíso's point of view," I commented to myself, "I'll bet I would be able to *feel* quite a wind right now created by all those wings!"

And what would I have been able to *hear* had the Power of Paraíso allowed it? Several times, I saw criados talking amongst themselves (the two sitting on the rafters appeared to be in the middle of a lengthy conversation) and, a few times, talking once again to invisible beings. I wondered if it was more sombras, and I wished I could see them. Two different times during my visit to the mall, I saw what appeared to be a fairly intense fight break out between the criados and the invisible sombras. During one of the fights, the two criados on the rafters swooped down to help out—battling with their mighty swords. I wondered if this was the war Risa had told me about.

I looked up at Fuego. He was walking along beside me on my left with his left hand resting on his sword. I looked up at his face: his red beard revealed no trace of a smile.

Suddenly, a thought came to me: *I wish one of those sombras would come over here,* I thought with a grin. *That would be cool to see someone get into a fight over me!* I wouldn't realize until later how cruel this thought actually was.

As our trip to the mall was drawing to a close, we swung by the restrooms to make a quick stop before heading for home. Aunt Sarah and I went one way and Jaime went the other. When I was finished, I came out of my stall (Fuego had guarded me from *outside* the stall, thank goodness) and I started for the sinks to wash my hands.

When I saw where I was headed, I stopped: there were mirrors over there. I had tried very hard all week to avoid mirrors; I didn't want to have to concern myself any longer with that stupid belt! I couldn't *feel* the belt, of course, so that made it pretty easy to ignore. But mirrors made ignoring it impossible.

Just then, Aunt Sarah came out of her stall. Without thinking, I went ahead and walked over to a sink—careful to keep my eyes down. After all, I didn't have to look in the mirror in order to wash my hands, did I?

I was doing fine until I saw a light reflecting from the mirror so brightly that I couldn't help but look up. There, covering my torso from my neck down to my belt was a silver breastplate—the piece of armor that knights wear in battle to protect their heart. It was beautiful...reflecting the bathroom light so brilliantly that I practically had to squint in order to look at it. I was amazed, but—after the belt experience—I can't say that I was all that surprised.

What was that on the breastplate, another letter? I leaned up closer to the mirror; there, over my heart, was a beautifully-written upper-case "R". I reached up and traced the letter with my finger. In real life, I was running my finger along the boring fabric of my t-shirt; in my reflection, my finger was presently inside a groove in the shape of the letter "R" engraved into a metal breastplate. I found myself wishing that I could feel it in real life.

I looked up; Aunt Sarah was watching me.

I dropped my hand and cleared my throat. "You know," I said, going back to washing my hands, "I think I might have gotten some food on my t-shirt when we ate a little while ago."

Aunt Sarah only smiled.

When we arrived home, we found a note from Dad and Uncle Antonio saying that they had gone to the video store and would be back soon. It was probably my dad's idea.

"Let's watch TV!" Jaime exclaimed, running to push the power button on the television set and then flopping down two feet in front of the screen.

I sat down in Uncle Antonio's easy chair. "Anything but cartoons, Jaime," I said.

He made a face.

I quickly noted that the show on the screen was not a cartoon; in fact, it didn't look like a "kid show" at all. *So this is what my dad was watching,* I thought to myself. "Jaime, change the channel," I said casually. "Let's see if something better is on."

"Wait a minute," he insisted.

I waited, but things didn't improve. "Jaime, change the channel," I repeated more forcefully. "This show isn't good for you." I started looking for the remote.

"What's the big deal?" he said, not turning from the screen. "It's just a *movie.*"

"It's a movie you shouldn't be watching, Jaime," I responded with agitation. "Now get up and change it *now!*"

"Okay, okay," he said, and *very* slowly made a move to change the channel.

Suddenly, I saw something else move: I looked to my left; Fuego was standing there guarding me, like usual. But for the first time, he had removed his left hand from the hilt of his sword and was now holding it in his right. The sword was long and wide and silver—and *very* intimidating.

I looked up at Fuego's face; the look in his eyes filled me with fear. Where had I seen that look before? It was a look of anger mixed with annoyance. Then I remembered: it was the look he'd had when he'd spotted the sombra across the room.

I followed his gaze: *He was looking directly over by where Jaime was sitting!*

Before I knew what I was doing, I jumped out of my chair, ran over to the television set and began to push every button imaginable in an attempt to turn it off. I finally found the right one.

"What's *wrong* with you?" I screamed into his face, grabbing him by the shoulders. "Didn't you hear what I *said?* I said *change the channel!* Why don't you ever *listen* to me, Jaime? Next time I say change the channel, you change the channel, do you understand me?"

Jaime quickly nodded, a terrified expression on his face.

I jumped up from the floor and headed for his room—slamming the door behind me. I fell down on the bed and covered my head with the pillow. "What's *wrong* with me?" I asked myself indignantly. "Why did I yell at him like that? Since when do I care what Jaime watches? It was only a TV show. It's not like the kid was in *danger*, or anything."

CHAPTER 20

The Mentor

"What's happening to me?" I asked myself out loud, staring at the bottom of the bunk above me. "I must be going crazy, or something. The kid didn't do anything wrong—why did I yell at him?"

I lay there on the bed—griping myself out for being such a jerk. Then I spotted the Book of Light.

"Let's see if the *book* can tell me," I said disdainfully, leaping off the bed. "If it has all the answers, then *it* can tell me!"

I flung the book open and started reading. (I was so angry that I didn't even notice that, for the first time, the light didn't hurt my eyes at all.)

Finally, be strong in the King and in his mighty power. Put on the full armor of the King so that you can take your stand against the enemy's schemes. For our struggle is not against flesh and blood, but against the rulers, against the authorities, against the powers of this dark world and against the spiritual forces of evil in the heavenly realms. Therefore put on the full armor of the King, so that when the day of evil comes, you may be able to stand your ground, and after you have done everything, to stand.

"I've read this part before," I mumbled, hunched over the desk. "Isn't this the part about the belt?"

I kept reading.

Stand firm then, with the belt of truth buckled around your waist . . .

"Yep."

I read on.

. . . with the breastplate of righteousness in place . . .

I shoved the book so hard that it bounced off the wall and landed a few feet from the desk.

"What's going on here?" I screamed at the book from a safe distance away. "You're just a book! You're just a stupid *book!* How did you know . . .?"

I stood there trying to catch my breath, one hand steadying myself on the chair. I looked down at the book; it had fallen facedown, so the light coming out of it was barely visible.

It looked so powerless laying there—an old book with torn cover and wrinkled pages. But looks can be deceiving. Something, or some*one*, was controlling that book. It was as if someone else were turning its pages and causing me to find the exact passages I needed to read! But how was that possible?

It was the King's book. Maybe he could do with it what he pleased.

I tried fitting this into the worldview I'd already created for myself, but it didn't seem to fit in anywhere. It didn't make sense no matter *how* I looked at it. I used to think I could gain control over any hard-to-understand situation if I just studied it long enough. It seemed the more I studied this book, the *less* in-control I felt.

Slowly, I approached the book and—with trembling hands—picked it up. I wasn't as afraid as I was in awe; I had found something that *worked.* Now I had two choices: I could either choose to accept it as true or reject it as coincidence. But one thing was for sure: I couldn't ignore it.

Luckily, I hadn't lost my place. The Book of Light had fallen facedown on the very page I had been reading. I gently smoothed out the wrinkled page and picked up where I had left off:

Stand firm then, with the belt of truth buckled around your waist, with the breastplate of righteousness in place, and with your feet fitted with the peace that comes with being ready to share the Book of Light with others. In addition to all this, take up the shield of faith, with which you can extinguish all the fiery darts of the evil one. Take the helmet of salvation and the sword of Espíritu, which is the Book of Light. And speak to the King in the power of Espíritu on all occasions with all kinds of thanks and requests. With this in mind, be alert and persistent in your requests for all warriors everywhere.

I stopped reading, but I kept looking down at the book. I didn't want to leave the light.

Then I did something that would change my life forever: I chose to accept the book as true.

Very carefully, I closed the Book and set it back on the desk. I walked over to Jaime's mirror and ran my fingers over the invisible "R" inscribed on my breastplate.

"Righteousness," I smiled.

If my theory was correct, there would be much more armor to come.

With my newly-made decision, I suddenly found myself wanting to know all about the Book of Light. To satisfy my curiosity, I took my questions to the only person I knew of who seemed to know anything about it: Aunt Sarah.

I found her in her room. "I don't know what other people do, Sara," she smiled, motioning for me to come and sit beside her on her bed, "but I'll tell you what I do when I'm reading the Book of Light: Besides using bookmarks, I use a highlighter to highlight the different sections that seem to 'speak to me.' Do you know what I mean by that?"

I told her I thought I did.

"That way," she continued, "the passages will stand out and be easier to find next time." She handed me a highlighter from off the top of her desk.

"There's a part in there, Aunt Sarah," I told her, taking the highlighter from her, "that describes the Book of Light as a sword. Do you know what that means?"

"Do I know what that means," Aunt Sarah laughed. "Honey, I've been there, done that. And you will, too, if you go on like you are."

"What do you mean?" I asked.

"Sooner or later," she explained, "Mentiroso will attack. When he does, the Book of Light will be your sword."

She had said this very matter-of-factly—as if it didn't bother her in the least to talk about fighting the leader of the sombras. "Mentiroso? You've *fought* him?"

"Sure have," Aunt Sarah nodded.

"Wow!" I couldn't imagine Aunt Sarah *ever* getting into a fight with *anybody*—much less the leader of an army!

"Of course," she shrugged, "I'm really not the one who won the battle—the King did. I was just his helper."

"I wish I could have been there!" I exclaimed. "Wasn't it scary?"

"Sure it was," she replied, "but I knew I would win. You see, Sara, the sombras are limited—even Mentiroso. He can't harm a member of the King's family who asks the King for help. The King's sons and daughters are protected by criados, so Mentiroso would have to fight his way through them first. But I'll let you in on a little secret, Sara: Mentiroso doesn't even *like* to have to fight! He would rather sit back and watch you defeat *yourself*. How do we defeat ourselves? By choosing to walk *right* into one of his traps. What do Mentiroso's traps look like? They come in all different sizes and shapes, but they usually center around a lie and they always cater to the one who's being trapped. What he'll typically do is first of all figure out what your weaknesses are. Then he'll post something along the road that will distract you and tempt you to veer off the path. It may not even be something bad, Sara; it could be something that is perfectly good. But it will always be *wrong*. Never trade, Sara, what is best for something that is merely *good*. As a child of the King, the entire Kingdom of Paraíso belongs to you. Never settle for less."

I sat there in silence, looking at Aunt Sarah. I realized for the first time just how cunning Mentiroso really was (and how smart Aunt Sarah was for figuring him out).

"Aunt Sarah," I said finally, "I don't *ever* want to have to fight Mentiroso. But if I *do* have to, how will I win? With the Book of Light?"

"That's right. Here," she said, leaning over and pulling open her desk drawer. "This a smaller version of the Book of Light that you can carry with you at all times. If you ever feel like a sombra is nearby, just quote him a verse or two— that usually puts him on the run. I advise you to memorize some key verses in there. You never know, they might come in handy some day."

I thanked Aunt Sarah and asked her why the Book of Light was so effective. What was it about it that scared the sombras so much?

"That's a very good question, Sara," she smiled, placing a hand on my shoulder. I didn't scoot away. "The sombras aren't actually afraid of the Book of Light in and of itself. What they're actually afraid of is the one who *wrote* the Book: the King. In fact, Sara, do you know what scares the sombras more than *anything*?"

"What?" I asked eagerly.

"The name of the Prince."

I waited for her to go on, but she didn't. "That's it?" I

121

asked in amazement. "Just a name?"

"It's not 'just a name,' Sara—it's the name of the *Prince*. Remember, it's the Prince who made it possible for you to live forever in Paraíso. If the Prince had not come, you would still be chained to a future in darkness. You would still be chained to the old life you used to live, and you would have no hope whatsoever for a better future. Because of the Prince, you do. Every time you speak his name, the sombras are reminded of this and shudder. 'If the Son has set you free, you are free indeed.'"

I looked at Aunt Sarah and smiled. Now I knew what made her eyes sparkle.

CHAPTER 21

The Shadow

I don't know if the breastplate of righteousness I was wearing had anything to do with this, but I suddenly found myself being nicer (not *nice*—just nic*er*) to Jaime. I agreed to go to a couple of his ball games (he was the first baseman on his tee-ball team), I played catch with him a few times in the front yard, and I even agreed to go with him to the local park now and then.

One of our trips to the park turned out to be more eventful than the usual climbing across the monkey bars and swinging on the swings. It started out normal enough: Jaime begged his mom to go, Aunt Sarah said "yes," Jaime begged *me* to go, I said "whatever," and the three of us got in the Suburban and went.

It was already nearing dusk when we got there, so Aunt Sarah told Jaime he wouldn't be able to play too long. Like always, Aunt Sarah would sit in the Suburban and watch us from there. We were to be careful and, of course, I was to "keep an eye on him." (Sometimes I wondered what Aunt Sarah did the rest of the year when I wasn't around.)

Night was falling, and the shadows were getting long.

Some parks have a lighting system that comes on at night so that kids can continue playing after dark. This park didn't have one; I wished it did.

"I'll race you to the swings!" Jaime called out, running on ahead of me. I let him beat me—mainly because my preferred speed was a slow walk.

I chose a swing and settled onto the black plastic seat. I have to admit, I like to swing. I always have. It's such a freeing feeling being so high up in the air—feeling your hair blowing back in the wind, the breeze brushing your face. In fact, before my ride on Espíritu, I'd always thought of swinging as the closest thing to flying.

In no time at all, Jaime lost interest and took off for the jungle gym. He called for me to join him, but I was quite content to remain where I was, thank you.

From high up in the air, I looked out over the horizon— or what I could see of it. This particular park was surrounded on three sides by trees. This made the park appear inviting to most, but to me it seemed a little intimidating. I felt trapped inside it like a bird in a cage—with some cat lurking around somewhere waiting to pounce on me. I always felt like somebody could be hiding behind one of those trees watching me. I know it's silly, but...

What was that? Oh, just a shadow. Why was it that things at night always seemed scarier than they did during the day? I'd never been to this park during the day (we always came in the evenings when it wasn't as hot), but I'm sure I would have thought the park was beautiful in the light of day. As it was, though, the menacing shadows cast by the trees...

There it was again. I'd slowed my swinging, and now I brought the swing to a complete stop. I looked across the park at the trees. They were pretty far away, but not far enough. *I'm sure it was only my imagination*, I thought to myself. *No one is hiding in those trees.* But I wasn't convinced. It was warm out here, so why was I getting chills?

Maybe the shadow was from a tree swaying in the breeze, I thought. But there was no breeze. The air was very still tonight.

"Sara, come play with me!" Jaime called from the jungle gym.

Slowly and mechanically, I stood to my feet. I didn't take my eyes off the shadow—which now appeared to have stopped moving. It wasn't the only shadow among the trees, of course; there were many others around it. But this shadow was different from the others: This was the only shadow that had moved. And this shadow wasn't shaped like a tree.

I walked slowly over to the jungle gym—my eyes not leaving the trees. In fact, I walked right into the metal bars of the jungle gym.

"Watch where you're going!" Jaime laughed.

I hardly heard him. I had seen the shadow move again. I felt my heart leap in my chest.

"Hey, Sara, climb up!" Jaime called down to me from atop the dome-shaped jungle gym.

I decided that wasn't such a bad idea; I might be safer up there. I climbed up. The bars were pretty far apart, so I was careful to get my footing so that I wouldn't fall.

I climbed up rather quickly, and Jaime thought that I was chasing him. He giggled and scampered down the other side to try and get away from me. By the time I'd reached the top, he was off and running—*straight towards the trees!*

"Jaime, stop!" I yelled at him.

He stopped only yards away from the shadow. "C'mon!" he called from across the park. "Come chase me!"

"Jaime, run away!" I screamed at him. "There's someone over there! Get away!"

He only thought I was playing and continued to stand there—waiting for me to come and chase him.

I didn't know what to do. I did the first thing that came

to mind and started to climb down quickly. But I lost my footing and fell between the bars—landing face-down on the grass with a thud.

For some reason, the fall didn't hurt as badly as it should have—or even knock the wind out of me. I looked down: For the first time ever, I could see *and* feel the breastplate on my front and the belt around my waist! I thought this was odd, of course, but I didn't have time to think about it: Jaime was in trouble.

"Jaime!" I called again.

Just then, I saw a bright flash of light. Fuego was standing right next to Jaime! (It's a good thing Jaime couldn't see him; he would have been scared to death!) His sword was drawn and outstretched. Through the bars, I watched as Fuego advanced towards the trees. I held my breath. What was he after? Who was hiding in the trees? From inside the jungle gym, I now felt caged-in more than ever.

Suddenly, a voice shattered my trance. "Jaime. Sara. It's time to go."

It was Aunt Sarah. Her voice wasn't loud, but it made me jump. I looked over my shoulder; Aunt Sarah was calling to us from inside the Suburban.

I turned quickly back to Jaime. He was running towards the Suburban—smiling from ear to ear. I looked beyond him; both Fuego and the shadow were gone. Whoever was hiding in the trees had apparently disappeared.

I looked down; my armor had also disappeared.

I crawled through the bars of the jungle gym and headed for the safety of the Suburban where Aunt Sarah and Jaime were waiting. I decided I wouldn't make any more trips to this particular park for a while—at least not at night.

CHAPTER 22

Jaime

I *wonder why my dad never talks to me*, I thought as I lay on my back looking up at the sky. There is nothing more enjoyable in life than watching the sky. The conditions were perfect: the day wasn't too hot, the birds were singing, and the clouds were beautiful. I knew from my school science class what kind of clouds these were: They were cumulous clouds. There are all different kinds of clouds, and cumulous clouds are the ones that people try to see shapes in. They're also the ones that can eventually turn into rain clouds. And they're the ones that drift silently along—strong and powerful—carrying your problems away with them. It was for this latter reason that I was watching them today.

It's been almost a month since we've been here, I continued in my mind. *I figured Dad would come around eventually. He usually talks more here. This trip, though, he hasn't talked much to anybody—not even to Uncle Antonio.*

The hard wooden floor was getting a little uncomfortable, but this was still my favorite place to come and think. A year ago, Uncle Antonio had begun building a treehouse for Jaime—but he'd never finished it. He'd gotten the floor done and the four walls, but not the roof. When I discovered the unfinished treehouse a few days ago, I took to it immediately. Here I could be alone and away from everything—and yet I could still see the sky. (Fuego allowed me the privacy I needed by finding a very large branch to sit on outside.) This treehouse was quickly becoming my favorite "thinking spot."

I'd had a lot to think about lately. I'd thought about why I was able to feel my armor at the park that day, and why I hadn't been able to feel it since. I'd thought about the shoes of peace (the next piece of armor listed in the Book), and wondered when they would come. I'd thought about my dad and why—ever since I'd become a warrior—I'd had a stronger desire than ever to try and get him to talk to me. And I'd thought about how Jaime was really growing up; he wasn't nearly as annoying as he used to be.

I heard movement down below and the sound of someone's struggle to climb the wooden ladder. I sighed. Jaime was coming up.

"Hi, Sara!" he said, flashing me that annoying smile of his. He was trying to pull open the treehouse's wooden door.

I didn't move except to give the door a push.

"Thanks!" he said, crawling in next to me. He turned around on his knees—his feet in my face—and pulled the door closed. Then he proceeded to sprawl out on the floor next to me with his hands under his head—fingers interlocking. It was the exact position I was in. Not long ago, I would have viewed this move as annoying. Now I thought it was kind of cute.

He lay there next to me for the longest time. Then finally I heard his little voice pipe up. "Sara?" he asked.

"Yeah?" I responded.

"What are we looking at?"

"The clouds."

"The clouds?"

"Yeah."

"Oh."

We lay there in silence.

"Sara?"

"Yeah?"

"Why do you like being by yourself so much?"

It was a question I was not prepared for. I shifted my position on the floor. "I don't know," I said, feeling my palms getting sweaty beneath my head. "I . . ."

I really didn't know. Why *did* I like being by myself so much? It would be something else to think about.

"I guess being by myself gives me time to think," I said.

"Think about what?" Jaime asked.

Normally, this was where I would tell Jaime to be quiet or to stop asking so many questions. But, like I said, being a warrior of the King was having a strange effect on me.

"Oh, different things," I heard myself say. "I like to think about flying." As soon as I said it, I blushed. Jaime would surely laugh at me.

Surprisingly, he didn't. Instead, he paused for a moment. "Me, too," he said dreamily.

I turned to look at him. "Really?" I asked.

"Yeah," he smiled, gazing up at the sky. "Just like that bird up there." He pointed straight up.

I looked up. Through the branches, I could make out a hawk or an eagle as it soared effortlessly along on the wind. It made me wish for another ride on Espíritu.

"Have you ever wondered," Jaime continued, "what it would be like to be able to fly like that—way up high, above everything? I mean, just think about it! You could look down at the people and the houses and I'd bet they would look like teeny tiny ants." He demonstrated the size with his fingers. "Everything would look so small from up there, wouldn't it?" he asked, looking at me.

I swallowed. I felt my eyes well up with tears. *That's what I want,* I thought, *for everything to look so small.* "Yes, it would," I almost whispered. I fought back the tears; I would *not* cry around Jaime.

I cleared my throat. "You know," I said, preparing to change the subject, "it's been a while since we've gone for a ride. What do you say we saddle up a couple of the horses tomorrow and go for a ride?"

His reaction was predictable. "Really?" he asked, bouncing up and down, his arms and legs flailing. "Yea!"

"Will your mom and dad let us go by ourselves?"

"Probably," he exclaimed, still bouncing, "as long as they can still see us and you're there with me, I'm sure my mom will say it's all right!"

I thought about it. Yes, Aunt Sarah probably *would* say it's all right.

"Jaime," I said, turning my head to face him, "now it's my turn to ask *you* a question: If you could have anything in the whole wide world, anything at all (besides being able to fly), what would you want?"

Jaime wrinkled up his nose and closed one eye—demonstrating that he was thinking very hard. After a minute of thinking, he said, "I think I'd wish for you to be my sister. I know I've *got* sisters, but I never even get to see them because they're so much older and they live so far away. You're more like a sister to me because you're around more and you do stuff with me—like ride horses and go to the park and play catch. Mom and Dad do stuff with me, but it's not the same thing, you know? You're somebody I can really *talk* to. Sometimes it's nice just to have somebody around to talk to, you know what I mean?"

I didn't attempt to hide the tears I felt in my eyes. Instead I looked at Jaime, and for the first time I saw more than a cousin: I saw a friend. "Yes, I do," I smiled.

CHAPTER 23

The Shoes of Peace

I decided the only way to solve the problem with my dad was to confront him one-on-one and explain to him the way I felt. It wouldn't be easy, but it was the only way. I had to do something; doing nothing had so far accomplished nothing. Besides, I wanted a chance to let him know about the Book of Light. Who knows? Maybe reading the Book of Light would change his perspective on some things.

My opportunity came one day while Jaime was gone to one of his ball games with his parents. I told Jaime I was sorry, but I couldn't go watch him today; I had something important that I had to do.

I found Dad sitting in his usual spot in front of the TV— holding a newspaper. I would have a double barrier to get through today. I looked to Fuego for help, but he rendered no assistance; I was on my own for this one.

I walked slowly over to the couch and sat down. I didn't know exactly how to start. I felt nervous. For most kids, it's easy to talk to your parents. Not for me. I could say one wrong thing and my dad would walk out of the room and the conversation would be over. I didn't want things to end up the same way they did last time. *I will* not *mention the word "church,"* I told myself.

"Dad?" I said, my voice breaking.

His eyes didn't move from the paper in his hands.

I cleared my throat and gathered up the courage to try again. "Dad?" I repeated, a little bit louder.

"What is it, Sara, I'm busy," he growled.

You're always *busy*, I thought. Okay, what could I say to get the ball rolling? *Dad, how come you never talk to me?* probably wouldn't be the best beginning line.

I searched my mind for a good conversation starter. "How are the teams doing this year?" I endeavored.

He gave me a strange look; he knew I couldn't care less about his sports teams. I smiled, hoping to fake him out. He didn't smile back. Instead, he turned back to his paper and said nothing.

Okay, so conversation starters didn't work. I decided to go with my original plan. "Dad, how come you never talk to me?"

He looked at me. He reached for the remote, muted the TV, put down his paper, and looked at me. Wow, that worked!

"Because," I continued quickly, looking down at the floor, "I remember how you used to talk more—a long time ago, before Mom died—and now you don't really talk that much. And I just wondered why."

I held my breath and awaited his response. I didn't know what to expect: fire or brimstone. I had never brought up my mother around him before.

Surprisingly, he sighed a deep sigh and—wonder of wonders—turned the TV off! Then he looked at me with eyes I'd never seen before and said, "Sara, your mother was a wonderful person."

Well, he hadn't answered my question, but at least he was talking. "Yes?" I encouraged.

His eyes shifted all around then looked down at his hands.

Come on, Dad, you can do it, I urged him in my mind.

I was starting to think he wasn't going to say any more when he finally came out with, "She . . . she was a good person—your mother was."

It looked as though he was going to need a little help. "What made her a good person?" I probed.

This brought an unexpected result. He looked up at me and did something I hadn't seen him do in a long, long time: he smiled. "She was always doing stuff for people—" he said to me, and then stopped. That old look came back into his eyes, and he clammed up.

No! It wouldn't stop here—not now that I was finally making some progress! "She was always doing stuff for people . . ." I prodded.

"I'm kind of busy right now, Sara," he said, turning the TV back on and picking up the newspaper.

I sat there, stunned. It would end here, like this? No! Not if I had anything to do with it. "Also, I was wondering," I said, unable to restrain my frustration any longer, "how come we don't go to church anymore."

He immediately reached for the remote again. "I told you, Sara," he said muting the TV, "we will *not* discuss that topic! It is not—"

"Because I was just thinking," I continued on, looking anywhere but at his eyes, my voice no longer meek and mild, "we used to go to church all the time before Mom died, and now we never go anymore."

"I don't want to discuss this, Sara!"

"I think it wouldn't hurt to start going again..."

"Sara—"

"At least then we would be *doing* something!"

"Sara, did you not hear me?" my dad shouted at me. "I do *not* want to talk about this!"

"That's your *problem*, Dad!" I shouted back. "You never want to talk about *anything*!"

In an instant, my dad was out of his chair—not even bothering to put down the leg rest. He thrust a finger in my face, then—using a tone of voice I'd never heard from him before—said, "You shut your face, do you understand me?"

I looked at his eyes. They looked strange—almost inhuman, as if a wild animal were controlling him. I'd never before imagined my dad hurting me, but at that moment I thought that he might—and it scared me.

I felt my own eyes fill up with tears. I scrambled away from him and fled the room.

When I reached the bathroom, I slammed the door behind me and locked it. I stood there for a moment—trying to catch my breath.

I was just as angry as I was scared. Why did my dad have to *be* this way? Why couldn't I have a normal conversation with my dad—just like every other kid on the face of the planet?

I clambered up onto the countertop next to the sink and pulled my legs up close. I was still trying to fight off the tears; other people cried, I didn't cry. Crying was for babies, and I wasn't a baby.

I started crying, then found I couldn't stop. I began to sob uncontrollably, my head against my knees. All the pain, all the anger that had been building up over the years was finally coming out, and there didn't seem to be a blasted thing I could do about it. I cried for my Dad. I cried for my Mom. I cried for myself.

When the tears were finally beginning to slow a bit, I looked in the mirror beside me. I looked awful. So *this* was why I never cried!

I looked at my armor. Although I had grown to appreciate it and even admire it, at that moment I hated it. Whatever it was that had happened to me, it had come between me and my dad.

I looked down: Through blurry eyes, I could make out

something shiny resting on top of the counter. I blinked a couple times. There in my reflection—in addition to the belt and the breastplate and in place of my old ratty sneakers—were a couple of silver shoes. Each of them was engraved on the sides with the letter "P."

"'The shoes of *peace*,'" I observed bitterly. "So how come there's not even a *hint* of peace in my life?"

I hugged my legs closer, bowed my head, and continued to cry.

CHAPTER 24

The Uninvited Guest

Needless to say, things didn't get any better between my dad and me after that. My plan had backfired: I had gone into the situation hoping to make things better by telling my dad about the Book of Light, and I had only ended up making things worse. Why did I have to shoot off my mouth like that? What did I think that would accomplish?

It must have accomplished something, though, because my dad agreed to go with us over to a friend's house for supper a couple nights later instead of staying home and watching TV. Jaime was glad when he found out; he said this way we could all meet his best friend Christopher.

Christopher turned out to be a pretty nice kid—same age as Jaime, blond hair and blue eyes as blue as Jaime's. Christopher was on Jaime's tee-ball team, and that's where they'd met. Christopher had a fourteen-year-old sister named Karen, but she wasn't there. (She probably didn't want to be stuck babysitting a bunch of kids. I didn't blame her.) The family had a nice house—too nice for two rambunctious boys; we were escorted outside to play before supper.

The first thing I saw when I stepped outside was the large

trampoline in the backyard. I'd always wanted a trampoline, but Dad—being the practical person that he was—said that trampolines were "unnecessary." I was glad when I discovered that jumping on the trampoline was what Christopher had planned for us to do. We headed over to it and Christopher and Jaime pulled off their shoes and socks. Then they clambered their way up with some difficulty. (There was a stepstool on the ground they could have used, but they probably wanted to prove to me that they didn't need it.) I waited until both of them were up, then kicked off my shoes (I wasn't wearing socks) and lifted myself onto the metal part—sitting on it with my feet on the black part near the springs.

Christopher said it was the family rule that only one person could jump at a time. He politely told Jaime that he could go first (which was good since Jaime was already jumping anyway). When his turn was through, Jaime walked over to the side and took a seat next to me, smiling. In the middle of his turn, Christopher remembered that he'd gotten a new video game. They mutually decided to go inside and play it. Left alone, I took my turn on the trampoline—glad to have it without an audience.

This was my first time on a trampoline, but I took to it like I'd been jumping my entire life. I'd never been scared to try new things, and I'd never been scared of heights. In fact, I tried to see how high I could jump. (Once I got a little carried away and ended up too close to the springs. I was a little more careful after that). I quickly discovered that jumping on a trampoline is much like swinging: It makes you feel like you're flying.

The time was late evening, so it was beginning to get dark. (We would be having a rather late supper tonight.) From high up in the air I looked out over the horizon; the sun was beginning to set. All was beautiful and serene. If only to remain in the air amongst the beautiful colors of twilight forever.

I decided to try some "stunts." I tried falling to a sitting position and then bouncing back up again. When I'd aced that, I moved on to the knee-drop which is a maneuver that involves falling to your knees and then coming back up without using your hands. This was a little harder. Then I tried doing a complete turn-around in midair—bouncing and spinning so that I landed facing the opposite direction. That was fun, but it took some practice. The first time I tried it, I didn't make it all the way around and ended up falling on my face. But I've never been one to give up easily. Pretty soon I was doing them so fast that I was making myself dizzy. At one point I thought I saw a shadow move in the distance, but I was so dizzy that I couldn't be sure.

I continued in the new game I'd created. I paused for a moment to get my balance back, then worked my way up to a high enough bounce and began another series of turn-arounds. Half-way through the second one, I was almost sure I saw something move. Just when I'd made up my mind to stop spinning long enough to look, my feet went out from under me. What had I slipped on? I looked down: My feet were shod in metal shoes.

The shoes of peace! And the breastplate and belt were there, too! "Cool!" I said aloud. "I was wondering when I'd get to—"

Suddenly, I looked up: Standing no more than ten yards away from me was a shadow. It wasn't lying along the ground like a normal shadow does but standing upright—as if a person were standing there and all I could see was their silhouette. The shadow was solid black; I couldn't see through it at all. It was shaped like a person . . . a *very tall* person! And this "person" had wings—I could tell by the outline. (If I'd never seen a criado before and was not familiar with seeing wings on the back of an individual, I probably would have thought that what I was looking at right now was not wings at all but rather a long, dark cape.)

Maybe it was a criado. But if it was a criado, then why did I suddenly feel the urge to jump off this trampoline and run for my life?

The shadow took a step towards me. I jumped off the trampoline and ran for my life. I made it to the back sliding glass door, jerked it open, stepped inside, and quickly pulled it closed. I stood there for a moment—still holding on to the door handle—trying to catch my breath. I would be safe in here.

The shadow suddenly appeared outside on the other side of the glass! I gasped and took a step backwards. I backed into Christopher's mom. "Oh, hi, Sara," she said, smiling at me. "I didn't see you." Then she said, "Would you mind setting the table for me? Thanks, sweetie," and handed me something.

I looked up: The creature was still standing there. All of a sudden, it stepped *right through the glass!* I ran to the other side of the dinner table—nearly slipping on the tile floor in my metal shoes. When I reached the other side of the table (it felt like an eternity), I stood there bracing myself on the back of a chair—my heart pounding. I tried to scream, but my voice wouldn't work. I looked around: The adults were all getting ready for supper. They were oblivious to the fact that a giant monster was standing in the middle of the room!

What would it do? What would the black shadow do? It started moving again; I tried to run, but I felt frozen where I was. The giant walked over to where my dad was standing. *Oh, Dad, don't you see it?* my mind screamed.

I watched as the creature lifted its hands and reached for my dad's head with curled fingers. Were those claws on the ends of its fingers? The claws came to rest on top of my dad's head and then disappeared!

Just then, Dad looked up at me. "Sara!" he yelled. That same look came into his eyes that I'd seen on the day of our argument. "Christopher's mom asked you to set the table! Stop standing there and do it!"

A movement to my left caught my eye. It was Fuego's sword. He was advancing towards the shadow with rapid strides. The creature immediately turned its head to face him, but it did not remove its claws. Fuego held his sword to the shadow's throat and said something. I could not hear his words, of course, but I could see his lips moving. There was a pause, then Fuego said something else. Suddenly, the shadow violently jerked its hands off my dad's head—removing its claws. Dad appeared to have been going to say something else, but he seemed to change his mind now and walked over to check on the oven. I watched as Fuego escorted the dark shadow out by same way it had come in—his sword at its throat.

A loud clamor woke me from my dream-like state. I looked down: the silverware I had apparently been holding was on the tile floor next to my bare feet.

"Sara?"

I turned. All five adults in the room were staring at me.

"Sara, honey, are you okay?" Christopher's mom asked, laying a gentle hand on my shoulder.

I stood there for a moment longer—still trying to catch my breath. Then I slowly bent down and began picking up the silverware I'd dropped. I closed my eyes and found myself thanking the King. Then I stood back up and turned to look at them all. "I'm okay now," I assured them.

CHAPTER 25

Mom

I had seen a sombra. There was no question about that. That monstrous black shadow with wings and claws.

As I lay on my back in the treehouse on this cloudy gray day, I found that I had plenty to think about. My armor had shown up twice now. What was making it appear? If I could figure out what both times had in common, maybe I could answer this question.

Okay, the first time my armor appeared, I was at the park with Jaime. I discovered it was there right after I fell off the jungle gym. The second time was yesterday evening at Christopher's house. I was jumping on the trampoline and the armor showed up right before I saw . . .

The sombra. Maybe sombras made my armor show up.

But that couldn't be it. What about that day at the park? There was no sombra around then.

Or was there? What about that shadow I had seen over by the trees? At the time, it made me nervous just because I didn't know what it was. I thought a person was hiding behind one of the trees.

But what if it wasn't a person at all? What if it was actually a sombra?

A shiver ran up my spine at the thought of how close Jaime had been to it. Both times, Fuego had stepped in to save us just in time. I automatically thanked the King.

I paused. That was the second time I had talked to the King without even realizing it. Maybe I would be doing that a lot now that I was a warrior. Maybe that's what warriors *did*. Maybe that's what I was *supposed* to be doing more often than I was. After all, hadn't Fuego said that I was the King's daughter? That meant that the King was my father, right? Why *shouldn't* I talk to him? Don't fathers want their daughters to talk to them?

Most do. I shifted my position on the wooden floor; I suddenly felt uncomfortable. What if the King was like my dad? What if—when I tried to talk to him—he wouldn't really want to listen? What if he had better things to do? He was, after all, the King of the entire world. What if he simply didn't have time for me?

The thought scared me. I don't know why, but it did. Up until now, I hadn't really cared whether the King listened to me or not; the thought had never even entered my mind. But now—with the possibility of him *not* wanting to listen—I suddenly felt something I had never felt before: unimportant.

I couldn't stop the tear from trickling down my cheek. Who was I kidding? I'd felt unimportant before—practically my entire life. Come to think of it, I couldn't think of a time when I'd *ever* felt all *that* important.

Maybe before Mom died. Another tear trickled down. I reached up and wiped it away. I was a warrior. Warriors weren't supposed to cry, were they? I wasn't sure. All I knew was that I'd sure done a lot more crying *since* I'd become a warrior than I ever did *before*.

Mom. It had been a long time since I'd thought about her—I mean, really *thought* about her. For some reason, I had pushed my memory of her way back to the back of my mind. Now I wondered why.

I could see her clearly—as if it were yesterday: long, black hair—brown eyes so dark that they looked black. I smiled. She really was beautiful, wasn't she? What a contrast she was to that horribly white hospital room. I could feel her hand touching my face. It felt soft and warm. "Everything will be all right," I could hear her voice saying to me. "Dad will take care of you. I'm going away now to a better place. Take care of your Dad, will you, Sara? He will need your help."

She was wrong. Everything was *not* all right. Dad was *not* taking care of me. And Dad didn't need my help—I needed *his* help. I needed him to be the kind of father he was supposed to be.

I turned over on my side. If I was going to cry, I didn't want Fuego to be able to watch. He had once again chosen as his lookout spot a large branch in the top of the tree outside. This time he was visible through the open roof of the treehouse. I could see him sitting up there watching me. Usually, he was nice to have around. But sometimes having a bodyguard was just plain *annoying*.

As I turned over, I felt something poking my leg from inside my pocket. I reached inside my pocket and pulled it out. It was the smaller version of the Book of Light that Aunt Sarah had given me.

I sighed and turned it over in my hand. It looked much different from the other Book of Light. It was much smaller, of course, and much newer-looking; the cover was black leather and the title was written in beautiful golden letters: "The Book of Light." It even had a thin scarlet ribbon attached to the spine to serve as a bookmark.

Unlike the other version of the same Book, it was very appealing and I felt enticed to open it. With my one free hand (I was using my other hand to prop myself up), I slowly cracked it open and squinted my eyes in preparation for a blinding light. There might as well have been no light coming out of the Book at all, for the light that met my eyes didn't hurt in the least. I didn't even blink.

For a minute, I thought there must be something wrong. I shook the Book a couple times, closed it, and then banged it against the treehouse floor. (I know this sounds strange, but—because this is how I would treat a malfunctioning flashlight—I thought this course of action might cause the light to resume its normal brightness.) I opened it again. The result was the same: the light didn't hurt my eyes.

Maybe it was because this Book was smaller. Or maybe that wasn't it at all. Maybe I had finally grown accustomed to the light.

I smiled and looked at the open page, near my thumb. I wasn't at all prepared for what I would read:

For all who live by Espíritu's leading are children of the King. For you did not receive a spirit of fear when you became a warrior; you received Espíritu himself. You are now the King's very own child, adopted into his family—and you can call him "Father," or even "Daddy." Espíritu speaks to our hearts and tells us that we are the King's children. And because we are sons and daughters of the King, our future is one of royalty; we will live someday like princesses and princes in the Kingdom of Paraíso. All of the riches in his Kingdom will one day belong to us, just as they belong to the Prince at this present time. But if we will someday share in the Prince's glory, we must also be willing to suffer for a little while longer—just as the Prince also suffered.

The gray sky, heavy with clouds, finally produced rain. It fell silently and softly—washing the tears from my face. There was no lightning or thunder. Only rain.

And I continued to cry. I looked up. I saw Fuego still sitting there in the tree above me. The rain wasn't touching him at all—he was perfectly dry.

Except for his face. His face was wet like mine.

CHAPTER 26

The Story

There was starting to be a growing desire within me to study the Book of Light more. I admitted to myself that I hadn't been reading it like I should. Aunt Sarah had told me (and I had read in the Book of Light itself) that the way a warrior could win a fight with a sombra was by using the Book of Light like a sword. I didn't know exactly what that meant, but I knew I had to learn to do it. I had been caught off guard by a sombra twice before. It wouldn't happen again.

So one night, after everyone else was asleep, I slipped out of bed as silently as possible so as not to wake Jaime. I got down on my hands and knees and reached under the bed. I felt for what I was looking for, pulled it out, and carried it out of the room—taking up the highlighter from Jaime's desk on the way out.

I made my way out the front door and up the ladder of the treehouse. Once there, I removed the Book of Light from under my arm, opened it up, and began to read. I read slowly and carefully; I didn't want to miss a single thing that Espíritu had to say to me (because, apparently, Espíritu "speaks to our hearts"). I worked all night—highlighting there in the dark the parts that Espíritu brought to my attention. (Of course, if I had been reading any other book, I would have needed a flashlight. But I wasn't reading just *any* book; I was reading the Book of *Light*—which is its own built-in flashlight.)

The parts I read that I liked best were the parts that had to do with winning a fight against Mentiroso:

Submit yourselves, then, to the King. Resist Mentiroso, and he will flee from you.

Another part said this:

Be careful! Watch out for attacks from Mentiroso, your great enemy. He prowls around like a roaring lion, looking for some victim to devour. Take a firm stand against him, and be strong in your faith.

And this one was cool:

The Prince of peace will soon crush Mentiroso under your feet.

I finally fell asleep—my head resting on the pages of light. I dreamed of battles and sword fights and knights fighting dragons. In one of my dreams, I was one of the knights. The dragon had no power over me because I was fighting with the sword of Espíritu—the most powerful sword in the world.

When I finally awoke, it was to a bird chirping outside the treehouse. I slowly opened my eyes. For a minute I didn't know where I was (which tends to happen when one falls asleep in a strange place). I blinked a couple times and looked down. The Book had remained open all night, but the golden shaft of light exiting its pages seemed to have grown only stronger for it.

I looked up. The morning sun illuminated Fuego; he hadn't moved from his position in the tree. "How does he *do* that?" I asked myself. "How can he sit up there like that all night long?"

I sat stiffly up. (I guess sleeping in a treehouse takes some getting used to.) I looked once more down at the open Book and closed it—but not without some hesitation.

I made my way down the ladder and back into the house. I guess I was still pretty tired, or I didn't expect anyone to be up, or sleeping in a strange place had made me jumpy. In any case, I jumped when I saw Aunt Sarah. She was sitting there on the couch—looking at me and smiling. It was as if she had been *expecting* me to walk through that door. "Oh, hi, Aunt Sarah," I said. "You scared me."

She didn't say anything. She just kept looking at me and smiling.

Now, I was beginning to like Aunt Sarah. But I *didn't* like how she always seemed to know more about what was going on in my life than I did. I'm kind of a private person, you know. And right at that moment, I felt as though my privacy were being invaded.

I held the Book of Light to my chest and quickly made for Jaime's room.

"Which ones did you find?"

I stopped dead in my tracks, but I didn't look up. Somehow, though, I knew she was still smiling. I looked up. Yep, she was still smiling.

She patted the space on the couch next to her. "Have a seat," she said. *Just like Mensajero*, I remembered.

I walked hesitantly over to the couch and sat down next to her, but I kept my distance. I hoped she would do the same.

For a moment she didn't say anything. Then I heard that quiet little voice of hers repeat, "Which ones did you find?"

"Which ones *what*?" I asked irritably, not looking up.

"Which verses?"

I looked up at her face: She was *still* smiling. Her eyes were so bright—as if she were seeing right through me. I felt like she was.

I looked down and didn't answer. Why did Aunt Sarah

have to be so *annoying* sometimes?

I figured she would demand an answer. Instead, she gently placed a hand on the Book of Light I was holding in my lap. I gripped it tighter. She was *not* going to stick her nose into my private life. If she opened the Book, she would see the stuff I'd highlighted and know I had been reading it. Then, no doubt, she'd have about a million questions for me on what I thought of it or what I'd learned. What I'd learned or thought of it was none of her business. No, this Book was going *right* back under the bed—just as soon as I could get away from Aunt Sarah.

I shifted my position on the couch and tightened my grip on the Book. She *finally* removed her hand and placed it in her lap. "You know, Sara," she said, "being a warrior is about more than just fighting the enemy. It's about living like a warrior *all* the time—even when the enemy is nowhere around. It's about being noble and choosing to do right—even when you have permission to do wrong."

She paused, as if waiting for some kind of response. I gave her none but continued to look down.

She went on. "There is a story found in the Book of Light, Sara, that I think would be helpful for you to hear. A long time ago, a boy named Joseph lived in the land of Canaan with his father and brothers. Like you, Joseph was a warrior of the King, so he tried to always do what was right. But life was not easy for him. In fact, his brothers were so mean that they sent him off to a foreign country as a slave, and at one point Joseph even spent *years* in jail for something he didn't even do. You'd think that Joseph would have stayed mad for the rest of his life because of all that had happened to him, but he didn't. He kept a good attitude, and the King rewarded him for it. In fact, he made Joseph ruler over the *entire* country where he had been a slave! Once he was a powerful ruler, he could have paid his brothers back for what they did to him long ago; instead, he did the noble thing and forgave them. And not only did he forgive them, but he threw a party for them with a huge feast."

My fingers loosened their grip ever so slightly.

"Joseph suffered a *whole* lot in his life, Sara, but he didn't let it get him down," Aunt Sarah continued. "He forgave those who hurt him instead of staying angry with them. As a result, the King rewarded him by giving him a wonderful life full of happiness and friends."

My hands now lay relaxed on top of the Book.

Aunt Sarah paused for a moment before continuing. "Forgiving someone is one of the hardest things to do," she said, "but it's the *noble* thing to do. We *all* make mistakes, Sara, so we should be willing to forgive others when *they* make mistakes. When someone hurts us, we only hurt ourselves by not forgiving them because we end up making ourselves miserable. (That's supposed to be a *sombra's* job.) It's better to forgive the person and go on. If we don't, our anger for one person can turn into anger for *everyone*—and pretty soon we find ourselves wanting to be alone all the time."

I looked up at Aunt Sarah.

"Be noble, Sara," she said, looking me directly in the eyes. "Choose to forgive others, even when they don't deserve it. As warriors, we have a responsibility: to be proficient at loving others. Besides loving the King himself, this is our *main duty* as warriors of the King. You want to be an effective warrior and a good fighter? You want to learn how to win battles against Mentiroso? Start by learning how to forgive. The toughest battle you will ever face won't be against any sombra—it will be against yourself."

I looked at Aunt Sarah for a moment longer, then looked down at the Book of Light resting in my lap. Slowly and carefully, I picked it up and placed it in the hands of Aunt Sarah. I looked up at her face—gentle and wise. "Please show me where that story is, Aunt Sarah," I said.

CHAPTER 27

The Shield of Faith

On Saturday of that week, I went to a water park with Jaime and Aunt Sarah. The water park was located a few towns away, so the drive there was about an hour and a half long. This gave me plenty of time to think about the conversation I'd had with Aunt Sarah.

I knew *exactly* what Aunt Sarah had been hinting at: She wanted me to forgive my dad. She realized, somehow, that he wasn't the kind of dad that he should be. Well, forgiving my dad wouldn't come easily. After all, he had neglected me for *years*. He didn't *deserve* to be forgiven.

Come to think of it, though, I hadn't exactly been the ideal daughter, either. There may have even been times when he had *tried* to show me love, but I had pushed him away. Isn't it strange how sometimes the things we want the most are the very things we try the hardest to push away?

In any case, forgiveness wouldn't come overnight. But I decided that I would try.

Jaime had been to this particular water park several times, so he knew right where to go once we got there. The first ride he wanted to do was a slide called "The Tunnel of

Death"—a very long slide that twisted and turned its way to the pool of water down below. The slide was totally enclosed, so it was also totally dark—except for the spots of light shining through the small holes in the sides. Jaime said he got scared, but I didn't. It's hard to be scared of *anything* once you've seen a sombra.

At one point during our trip to the water park, I discovered that I needed to use the restroom. (One of the most *annoying* things in the world is to have to use the restroom in a wet swimsuit.) Aunt Sarah told me where the restrooms were, then she stayed with Jaime at the wave pool while I headed off in the direction she had indicated.

I don't know what it is about restrooms in water parks, but they always seem to be dimly lit. Maybe, since the doors are typically propped open to keep people from having to touch a wet door, somebody figured they could save on money by allowing the sunlight from outside to light the room. (I don't know *what* they do on cloudy days.)

This restroom was no exception, but I *did* notice something strange about it: Nobody else was there. Usually there's a long line in a place this big.

"Oh, well," I said out loud to myself. "I can take all the time I need in here now."

As soon as I was done, I went over to the sink to wash my hands. I looked in the mirror at my armor; it really was beautiful, wasn't it? Even in this room of low light, the breastplate and belt sparkled like sunlight on the water. (I couldn't see my shoes, of course, but I knew they were sparkling, too.)

I was just finishing drying off my hands when I decided to have some fun (since nobody else was in there) and try to "make a basket" with my wadded up paper towel. I shot... and missed. (I never *was* very good at basketball.)

I walked over to pick it up. I bent down and momentarily admired my sparkling silver shoes while I was down there. Then I picked up the paper towel and tossed it in the wastebasket.

Wait a minute. Had I just been admiring my *shoes*?

I did a double take and looked back down at my feet. The shoes of peace were sparkling like sunlight on the water.

But why was I able to see them? I wasn't looking in the mirror...

I ran over to a mirror; my hands flew to my torso—my armor had materialized and was now covering my swimsuit. I could both see *and* feel the belt, breastplate, and shoes!

I was excited at first, then suddenly I remembered: a possible reason for my armor showing up may be because a sombra is nearby!

I swung around—bracing myself on the sink behind me—my chest heaving in and out beneath my breastplate. I looked all around. *Is there a sombra in here?* The thought paralyzed me with fear. *It could be hiding in any* one *of those stalls!*

Suddenly, the dark room became even darker. I jerked my head in the direction of the doorway: standing there, blocking my only way out, was a six-and-a-half-foot shadow with wings and claws!

I let out a shriek and felt my feet slip out from under me (darn these shoes!) as I tried to run. Instinctively, I fled into the nearest stall. But I felt even more trapped than before, so I ran right back out again.

The sombra was still there—only closer.

"Help!" I screamed at the top of my lungs. "Can anybody out there hear me? *Help!*" There were surely people walking around just right outside the door—why couldn't they hear me? But even if someone *did* hear me, what could they do? They wouldn't be able to see the monster—not without the Power of Paraíso. They would likely just think I was crazy.

The monstrous black shadow was getting closer—I had to do something. I looked around the room for something I could use as a weapon; there was nothing I could use.

Or was there? The Book of Light could be used like a sword. Oh, if *only* I had it with me!

Wait. Maybe I did. Maybe just quoting from it would be enough. But I hadn't worked long enough on memorizing it—I only knew a few verses. I wasn't even sure if I remembered those...

The sombra was only a few feet away now. I had to try *something*.

"'The Prince of peace will soon crush . . .'"

I didn't finish quoting the verse because I didn't have to; the black shadow had halted dead in its tracks.

I held my breath. What was it going to do? Was it going to go away since I had quoted from the Book of Light?

My question was answered when the thing started toward me again. My mind raced—I quoted the entire verse from memory: "'The Prince of peace will soon crush Mentiroso under your feet.'"

It had stopped moving ever since the words "the Prince" left my mouth, but I wanted to make *sure* it wasn't going to start up again so I went ahead and finished the verse.

The creature seemed to be thinking about what to do—it didn't look nearly as brave as it had before. It looked more like a soldier in the middle of battle who was suddenly realizing that he had underestimated the power of the enemy.

I took advantage of this slight hesitation on the part of the sombra and decided to quote another verse I had learned by memory. "'Submit yourselves, then, to the King. Resist Mentiroso, and he will flee from you.'"

What was this? Was the black shadow actually *retreating?* There was no mistaking it: The giant sombra had actually taken a step *backwards!*

Yes! This was working! Let's see, what else did I know?

"'I command you—be strong and courageous! Do not be afraid or discouraged. For the King is with you wherever you go.'"

I had it backed up nearly to the doorway now. I was amazed to find myself standing in the middle of the room—had I actually been walking *towards* it?

"'Don't be afraid,'" I quoted again, "'for I am with you. Do not be dismayed, for I am your King. I will strengthen you. I will help you. I will uphold you with my victorious right hand.'"

I'd now come to the end of my memory verses, but I knew what scared a sombra more than anything: "I'm a warrior...a child of the King!" I shouted at the blackness. "Therefore, in the name of the Prince of Paraíso, I command you to—"

I didn't have to say "go" because it was already gone.

I stood there in the doorway—basking in the light of the sun. I turned to face the mirror next to me. My armor shone brilliantly in the sunlight, and I smiled.

What was that behind me hanging on the wall shining as brilliantly as my armor? I turned to look: it was a shield—magnificent and grand and bearing a calligraphic letter "F" so large that it covered nearly the entire surface of it.

The shield of faith.

I walked over and removed from the wall my newest piece of armor. (It wasn't too heavy for me to hold, but it wasn't light, either). "Thank you, King," I said, smiling—attempting to strap the immense silver shield onto my arm. (It was practically the length of my entire body!)

Just as I had the silver shield in place—and before I even had the chance to adjust to the feel of wearing it—my belt, breastplate, shoes, and shield vanished...leaving me to exit the room wearing a simple, uninteresting swimsuit.

CHAPTER 28

The Ball of Fire

I hadn't gotten far away from the water park restroom when my armor showed up again. *Oh, great,* I thought. *Not again. There is* no way *I am fighting that thing in public!*

I quickly looked around me to see if any of the passersby noticed anything different about me (namely that I was walking through a water park wearing a suit of armor). I was greatly relieved when no one seemed to notice the change.

I also looked around for the sombra. It was just beginning to get dark out here. At least in the restroom I'd had a little bit of light. The idea of having to fight a sombra in the dark didn't exactly thrill me.

Just then, I heard a cry for help. I started running in the direction of the sound (but not too fast so as not to slip and fall on the wet ground in my metal shoes). It sounded like it was coming from the wave pool—the place I had left Jaime and Aunt Sarah. When I reached the pool, I looked around. Everything seemed all right: The waves were turned on and everyone seemed to be having a good time floating up and down in their inner tubes. There was no sign of distress anywhere, and I didn't hear anyone yelling for help.

Just when I was beginning to think that it must have only been my imagination, I heard a very faint sound that could have been a cry for help. I looked around; where was it coming from? The sun was going down behind the wave pool, and a large wall near the deep end obstructed its view so that it seemed here to be darker and later than it had out in the open. I began walking towards the deep end hoping that my eyes would quickly adjust.

Then I heard it—louder this time: a distinct cry for help. I ran over to the side of the pool and looked down into the water. There in the deep end—clinging with all his might to the metal bar located along the side of the pool while at the same time doing his best to keep his head above the waves—was a small child with jet-black hair.

It was Jaime!

Jaime was not an experienced swimmer; what he was doing in the deep end I didn't know. All I knew was that he was in trouble, and I had to do something to try and save him.

My first impulse was to jump in after him. Then I remembered what I had been told about rescuing someone from drowning: "*Never* jump in after them; they'll only pull you down, too, and you'll both drown." (*Besides*, I thought to myself, *there's no way I could keep my head above the water in this armor.*)

I looked around for something I could use to reach down to him that he could grab a hold of—like a long pole or a life preserver. I couldn't see anything.

Then I looked up and saw the reason for why my armor had materialized: Standing on the opposite side of the pool, a tall, dark shadow silently kept watch.

I looked over my left shoulder; Fuego was keeping watch, too. I knew no harm would come to me because of him.

But what about *Jaime?*

"Look, Jaime's in trouble!" I suddenly shouted up at

Fuego. (This was the first time I'd attempted to speak with him since our conversation in the kitchen.) "Aren't you going to do anything? Help me pull him out!" I was surprised to find myself angry with him—as if Jaime's drowning were his fault. "Come on, don't just stand there—*do* something!"

Suddenly, the black shadow on the other side of the pool leapt into the air! Its enormous wingspan stretched about thirteen feet across—*twice* the size of its height! I dropped to the ground in sheer terror, covering my head with my arms. I looked up; the huge, bat-like creature was now hovering directly above me!

I looked to Fuego for help. "Do something!" I yelled at him.

He didn't take his eyes off the sombra; he was glaring up at it with a look of anger mixed with annoyance.

I followed his gaze to the sombra; the dark shadow hovered above me like a vulture about to partake of its prey. I cowered on the ground like a frightened animal—forgetting all about Jaime or that I was a warrior of the King and had authority over dark shadows.

When I felt a light tap on my left shoulder, I jumped. I looked up: Fuego had drawn his sword and was now holding it out so that the tip of it pointed to my left arm. What was he trying to tell me? I knew that criados were not allowed to speak to humans unless special permission was given them by the King. (In fact, criados are not allowed to interact with humans in *any* way unless special permission is given them by the King; Fuego must have asked for special permission.) I looked at him strangely. Was he trying to tell me something?

I quickly turned back to the sombra—too afraid to look away for long. The terrible black wings flapped in a steady motion (although, of course, I couldn't hear or feel the force of their flapping), and its outstretched arms revealed vulture-like talons on the ends of its fingers.

I felt another tap. I turned to Fuego, annoyed at him for continually trying to distract me. Whatever he needed to tell me, it couldn't be important enough for me to take my eyes off the black creature that was hovering above my head. Again, he was using his sword to point to something near my left arm.

"What *is* it?" I shouted up at him from the ground. "Jaime's in trouble—and now I am, too—and all you can find to do is to keep tapping me on the shoulder! Why don't you make yourself useful and fly up there and protect me, since that's your job, instead of just standing there like a useless statue!"

A hurt expression appeared on his face; Fuego's red beard fell. He silently resumed military position, leaving out his sword.

I turned back to the sombra, ignoring Fuego's reaction. If he was going to pout about it, that wasn't my problem. I wasn't sorry for what I'd said. If I'd hurt his feelings, then he was far too easily hurt—especially for a big guy with wings and a sword.

Just then, I saw what looked like a ball of fire fly through the air and skid across the water—nearly hitting Jaime in the head. I looked up: The sombra was holding in its taloned hand something bright and yellow—like a small sun. Flames leapt out from the surface of it.

I didn't have much time to study it before the sombra sent it spinning through the air—straight at my head! I ducked and instinctively covered my face with my arm. As I did, the shield on my left arm was automatically brought up to my face. I felt the force of the fireball as it hit my shield and bounced off—dropping into the water down below with a hiss. A second's delay and that would have been my face.

I looked up at Fuego: so *this* was what he had been trying to tell me—to use my shield!

I felt like a warrior again as I stood to my feet. For a

moment, the game of Nieve-nube flashed across my mind; I remembered the success I had had with it. Of course, this was no game, but perhaps the practice I'd had would do me some good. And I had something much more powerful than snow-clouds to use as ammunition this time. "'Submit yourselves, then, to the King,'" I shouted up at it. "'Resist Mentiroso, and he will flee from you!'"

The sombra responded by hurling its fiery ammunition even more violently than before. I blocked it with my shield of faith—careful to hold it in such a way so as to make sure the ball of fire wouldn't bounce off onto Jaime.

"'I command you—be strong and courageous! Do not be afraid or discouraged. For the King is with you wherever you go.'"

This time the sombra's ammunition missed me completely. It was losing concentration—and power.

I looked down at Jaime; he was still holding on. I would have to figure out a way to save him while at the same time saving myself.

Suddenly, I knew what to do: I wrapped my arms around a nearby lamppost (which had just a moment ago been turned on to provide the swimmers with more light) and dangled one of my legs down to Jaime for him to grab. I hoped it would reach.

"Here, Jaime, grab my foot!" I yelled down to him.

The sombra didn't waste any time: another fireball came sailing my way. But I had carefully positioned the shield so that it covered the length of my body, so the fire didn't touch me.

I felt Jaime grab a hold of my foot (or, actually, my shoe) as I hoisted him up. I don't know who was more scared and exhausted—Jaime or me.

"I was so scared, Sara," Jaime cried, tears streaming down his face. "I thought I was going to die!"

I looked up; the sombra was gone.

As I hugged Jaime close to me, I looked up at Fuego—silently keeping watch to my left. I smiled up at him. He knew what I meant and smiled back.

I hugged Jaime tighter—determined to hold him like this for as long as he needed it. "Me, too, Jaime," I said, kneeling with him in the light of the lamppost. "Me, too."

CHAPTER 29

The List

I figured out why Fuego didn't rescue Jaime that day at the pool: I had asked—or, rather, *demanded*—that he help me. What I should have done was make my request to the King. *After all,* I thought, *criados aren't servants of warriors; they're servants of the King. Fuego didn't listen to me because that's not his job. His job is to listen to the King*—not *the person he's protecting.* Perhaps if I had asked the *King* for help, the King would have instructed Fuego to give me a hand. That would have been nice.

I guess I would never know. But one thing I *did* know: I wasn't talking to the King like I should have been. I was reading from the Book of Light daily now (usually in the morning—up in the treehouse), but somehow it didn't feel like enough. Even though I was starting to know a lot *about* the King, I didn't know *him.*

I came to this conclusion one morning while in my regular reading spot. I'd just read something in the Book of Light that got my attention:

And now you also have heard the truth—the Good News that the King saves. And when you believed in the Prince, the King identified you as his own by giving you Espíritu, whom he promised long ago. Espíritu is the King's guarantee that he will give us everything he promised and that he has purchased us to be his own people. This is just one more reason for us to praise our glorious King.

It was this last sentence that got my attention. It was my duty (and privilege) as a warrior of the King to be always praising him. As I sat there and thought about it, there really *was* a lot in my life to be thankful for. I just hadn't ever stopped to think about it before.

Suddenly, an idea came to me: I wanted to write down all the things I was thankful for. I looked around the treehouse for something to write on. In the corner was the comic section of a newspaper that Jaime had brought up to read. I took it and tore off a comic strip (I would have to write around Snoopy and Charlie Brown) then looked around for something to write with. Since I couldn't find anything, I decided to use the highlighter I always used for highlighting verses in the Book of Light. These resources would have to do for now.

My list looked something like this:

Only come to visit here once a year
Live in eastern Texas instead of southern Texas
Got to ride white horse this summer
Got to ride white *flying* horse this summer
Survived sombra attacks
Jaime and me friends now
Mom didn't have to suffer long

The last one got me started thinking about Mom again. It's strange how—when you're in the middle of a situation—you can't always see the reason for it, but afterwards when you look back you realize that the event might have had a purpose. That's how it was for me now. *Maybe Mom died,* I thought to myself, *so that Dad and I would end up taking a trip down here to Uncle Antonio and Aunt Sarah's house every summer.*

I thought about this for a long time, then looked down at the list again.

"Thank you, King," I said, "for doing all this stuff for me. Thank you for always being there, even when I wasn't aware of it."

It felt a little weird—talking to someone I couldn't see. But in a way it also felt really cool—like I was finally doing what I was born to do.

I looked down again at the passage. It said that one reason to give thanks to the King was because he had given us Espíritu. *Wait a minute,* I thought to myself, *I don't have Espíritu. If I had Espíritu, I would have him hidden away in the barn with the other horses—taking him out once in a while for a ride.*

Then I remembered the verse I'd read before about Espíritu speaking to our hearts. I still didn't understand what that meant—maybe I would *never* understand. But I believed it, and maybe that was enough. Like the King, maybe Espíritu was right here with me, somehow.

The thought both excited and scared me (just like Espíritu himself). If Espíritu had been with me all this time—ever since I believed in the Prince—then that meant that I'd done and said a lot of things around him that I wasn't too proud of. (I was certain, of course, that the King had been with me from the very beginning—watching me and listening to me *long* before Espíritu ever showed up.)

I looked down at the Book:

I ask the King, the glorious Father of the Prince of Paraíso, to give you wisdom and understanding so that you may grow in your knowledge of the King. I ask that the eyes of your heart may be enlightened, that you may know the great hope to which he has called you—the glorious future that he has in store for you. May you begin to understand the incredible greatness of his power for us who believe in him. This is the same mighty power that raised the Prince from the dead and seated him in the place of honor at the right hand of the King.

"'May you begin to understand the incredible greatness of his power for us who believe in him.'" I read that part again. I decided right then and there that I didn't understand the King nearly as well as I had thought I did. The King was not only a Father to his children; he was also their power source.

Of course, this started me thinking about my armor and the war I was in. I had already gotten a taste of the King's power when I'd battled the sombras, but I wasn't satisfied. I wanted to be more familiar with this power of which the verses spoke.

I needed to know the King better, I decided. How could I do that? How do you get to know someone you can't see or hear?

As if in answer to my question, a thought came to me: I *could* see and hear him! What was it I had been doing not five minutes ago? Making a list of all the good things in my life and then thanking the King for them. Wasn't that evidence enough? Surely the blessings in my life had not come to me by accident. (I was far too practical to believe in coincidences.) I would get to know the King better by paying better attention to the blessings, and then remembering to thank him for them.

I don't know why, but I felt a smile creep its way onto my face. I liked the idea of someone else being in control of my life (*I* certainly hadn't done a good job of it so far), and I liked the idea of someone constantly watching me and listening to me (although I could hardly believe I was thinking this way). It made me feel safe, somehow...and it made me feel loved.

"King," I said to him, bowing my head over the open Book, "I want to get to know you better. Please help me to do that by talking to you more. And thank you for all of the blessings in my life."

I closed the Book of Light with the comic strip inside; it would serve as a bookmark. I left the treehouse that morning a more grateful person. And the day just *might* have been lived out a little differently because of it.

CHAPTER 30

The Helmet of Salvation

I was starting to meet with Aunt Sarah nearly every night to discuss my daily growth as a warrior. We would talk about the Book of Light and what we were each learning from it. (I found out that Aunt Sarah—even though she had been a warrior for a long time—still read from the Book of Light daily, as well.) I found myself constantly amazed at her wisdom; she always seemed to know *exactly* what I needed to hear. (I think Espíritu must have been telling on me.)

We also practiced what Aunt Sarah called "sword drills": she would tell me a verse and I would see how quickly I could look it up in the Book of Light. "No weapon formed against you shall prosper, Sara," she would tell me, "unless *your* weapon is dull." So we worked many nights to make sure it stayed sharp. We also worked a lot on memorization. I already knew several verses by memory, of course, but Aunt Sarah helped me by asking me to quote them to her and by encouraging me to write them out on note cards—reading them aloud daily. She also knew of additional verses that I was unfamiliar with.

Gaining wisdom and practicing sword drills weren't my

only reasons for meeting with Aunt Sarah, however. It was with her that I was learning how to speak to the King. She told me that there wasn't only one way to do it, of course, but that certain things were usually included—like praises and requests. She told me that I should be making requests concerning my dad in the name of the Prince. This was difficult for me, but I did it anyway. I asked the King to open his heart...and to save him.

With the help of Aunt Sarah, I was feeling pretty confident about my next sombra encounter. After all, the King was on my side, so who could be against me? (That was from a verse in the Book of Light.) I knew plenty of verses by memory now, so I had plenty of ammunition. The way I saw it, the next sombra who crossed my path wouldn't stand a chance. But pride comes before a fall (that was another one), and sombras tend to wait until your most vulnerable moment before making their attack.

I found this out the hard way one Saturday night at the movies. There was a movie I was just *dying* to see, but my dad said that it was "inappropriate" for me and that I should see a different one. Since when did my dad care what I watched? And since when was my dad a good judge on the "appropriateness" of movies? But because Aunt Sarah said that I should "honor my parents," I said okay and told him I would see a different one.

Aunt Sarah, Jaime, and I bought our tickets to the kiddy movie Jaime wanted to see. We bought our popcorn and sodas and then took our places in the theatre. After the two-dozen advertisements were finally over, the actual movie began. It was an animated feature about some woodland animals and the perils of a housing district that threatened to take over their home. It was a G-rated movie. (Aunt Sarah never allowed Jaime to go to a movie at the theatre unless it was rated "G.") I could tell instantly that it was going to be *completely* boring.

But I had a plan. About fifteen minutes into the movie, I told Aunt Sarah that I had to go to the bathroom and snuck into the theatre showing *my* movie. The movie had already started; that was okay with me. I waited for my eyes to adjust to the darkness, then went and found an empty seat. I looked around: the place was nearly sold-out. *It must be a good movie if so many people are here to see it,* I reasoned. Of course, there were no other kids in here, but I tried not to let that bother me. (I tried not to let the fact that the movie was rated "R" bother me, either.) My favorite actor of all time was in this movie; I was *not* going to miss it. So what if it was rated "R"? Did that necessarily mean it was a bad movie? So what if it had a little violence and bad language? It wouldn't be anything I hadn't seen or heard before.

For some reason, I couldn't get comfortable. I shifted around in my seat (probably distracting the other people around me). I thought I saw a shadow move across the theatre. It was dark in here. It could have been an actual person.

I decided I needed to use the restroom. Frustrated, I got out of my seat and made my way (past even more frustrated viewers) to the hall. Once in the bathroom, I slammed the door to the stall and sat down. Yes, I was angry because I was missing my movie. But I was angry for another reason, too: Ever since I'd entered that theatre, Espíritu hadn't left me alone. What a *bother* he could be sometimes!

As I continued to sit there and fume about it, some memory verses popped into my head:

Dear brothers and sisters, honor those who are your leaders in the King's work. They work hard among you and warn you against all that is wrong. Think highly of them and give them your wholehearted love because of their work. And remember to live peaceably with each other.

Now I was even madder. "What does that have to do

with *anything?*" I complained to Espíritu. "Who am I dishonoring?"

I wasn't expecting an answer, but Dad and Aunt Sarah came to mind.

"What?" I screamed at the stall door. "Are you *kidding* me?"

He wasn't kidding.

In irritation, I reached into my shorts pocket, pulling out the smaller version of the Book of Light that I'd gotten into the habit of carrying with me. "If that's *really* what you're telling me," I announced to him, "then make it open to that section."

I opened the Book and started reading.

Ha! It wasn't that section!

Unfortunately, it *was* a section that said practically the same thing:

Do not stifle Espíritu. Do not scoff at prophecies, but test everything that is said. Hold on to what is good. Keep away from every kind of evil. May the King of peace make you holy in every way, and may your whole spirit and soul and body be kept blameless until that day when our Prince—the Prince of Paraíso—comes again.

I sighed. Why did Espíritu always have to be right? I *knew* I wasn't keeping my whole spirit and soul and body blameless by going to that movie. I *knew* I wasn't. I had been lying to myself.

Then it hit me: by dishonoring Dad and Aunt Sarah, I was also dishonoring the King himself.

"I'm sorry, Father," I told him. "I didn't mean to dishonor you. And I didn't mean to dishonor Dad or Aunt Sarah, either. Will you forgive me?"

He said yes.

A burden now lifted from my shoulders, I was about to close the Book and place it carefully back into my shorts pocket when I happened to glance down at the open Book:

Dear brothers and sisters, I read, *honor those who are your leaders...*

This section was on the same page as the other.

I exited the stall and walked over to wash my hands. Resting on the counter was something bright and beautiful. It was a helmet. A helmet of salvation.

I picked it up and examined it. It was wonderfully crafted—a metal visor in the front to protect the knight's (or *warrior's*) face. Above the visor, the letter "S" had been engraved into the front of it.

I proudly put it on. As I did, the rest of my armor appeared. I stepped out of the bathroom; a sombra was standing outside the door. It watched helplessly as I made my way back to the theatre where Jaime and Aunt Sarah were enjoying their movie.

CHAPTER 31

Engaño

I knew the Book of Light well enough to know that the only piece of armor I was lacking now was the sword of Espíritu. This was the one I wanted most.

When we got back from the movie theatre, it was pretty late. After changing into my sleepwear, I headed for Aunt Sarah's room for our nightly study of the Book of Light. I knocked on the bedroom door.

"Who is it?" I heard a muffled voice ask.

"It's me, Aunt Sarah," I said.

"Just a second," replied a sleepy voice.

A few seconds later, the door opened a crack. Aunt Sarah was standing there in her housecoat—her long, blond hair hanging freely around her shoulders. "Yes?" she smiled sleepily.

"Are we going to have our Book study tonight?" I asked hopefully.

"Not tonight, Sara," she said with a yawn. I could hear Uncle Antonio behind her brushing his teeth in their bathroom. "It's late. We'll do it tomorrow, okay?"

"Okay," I said. I didn't try to hide the fact that I was

disappointed, but Aunt Sarah didn't seem to notice. She just quietly closed the door back.

Now what? I thought. I went to Jaime's room; he was already in bed and sound asleep. I lay in bed for about a minute, then got back up again. I couldn't sleep—not with the Book of Light on my mind. I retrieved the Book from under the bed and headed for the living room. After flicking on a couple lights, I flopped down in Uncle Antonio's easy chair for some midnight reading. I picked up where Aunt Sarah and I had left off—on chapter 13, a chapter that Aunt Sarah referred to as "the love chapter." (It was one of Aunt Sarah's favorites.)

A few minutes into my reading, a thought entered my mind: *Aunt Sarah's just being difficult,* I thought. *She could have gone ahead and had the study with me if she'd really wanted to. She must know about what I tried to do today at the movies, and this is her punishment.* The more I thought about this, the madder I got. Pretty soon, I found myself so distracted that I was no longer even reading the passage— nor remembering what I'd read.

A light in the kitchen caught my eye. I looked at it for a moment: someone had apparently left a candle burning. I got up to blow it out. I knew the dangers of leaving a candle burning all night.

As I neared the kitchen, I noticed that the flame didn't look much like a candle. It was bigger and rounder and it didn't flicker the way a candle's flame does. It glowed brightly with a consistent glow and flames leapt out from it like flames on the sun.

I stopped dead in my tracks. Where had I seen something like that before?

Suddenly, there was movement as I saw what appeared to be long, black fingers curled around the ball. I looked up: looming above me was a six-and-a-half-foot shadow.

I felt the Book of Light I was still holding fall out of my

hands and hit the floor with a thud. Very slowly, I began backing away—my heart racing. The sombra moved towards me. I backed into a chair and nearly fell, but I kept my balance. I tried to recall a verse from the Book of Light to use as ammunition, but nothing came to mind. It was like my mind was frozen. And the Book of Light was out of reach—lying on the floor in an open position, the way it had fallen. Light was pouring out of it.

I reached for my pocket—I didn't have a pocket. Then I remembered: I had already changed into my sleepwear. The smaller Book of Light wasn't available to me, either.

I looked to my left: Fuego was keeping watch not too far away. I knew that asking him for help wouldn't do any good; he wouldn't help me. I could ask the *King* for help, though. "Father, please help me," I breathed.

The sombra moved in a little closer. I was backed up against a wall now. My armor was in place, and I heard it clank as I hit the wall. The visor on my helmet made it difficult for me to see; I raised it. The sombra took a step closer to me and then stopped. For a moment, I wondered why. Then it occurred to me: the Book of Light was between us. A wall of light separated me from the sombra. The creature would come no closer because it would not come near the Book of Light.

I began to feel less afraid. "Get out!" I commanded. "You have no right to be here! I am a child of the King—the King of Paraíso! I am his daughter! You can't hurt me because I am protected by the King himself! So get out!"

The sombra made no move to leave but continued to stand there, silently holding its fireball.

Then I remembered something: On that day when I first met Fuego, a sombra had appeared in the living room—not far from where I was standing now. I could not yet see it, but Fuego could and he had referred to it by name—and it left. What had he called it?

Engaño! Its name was Engaño!

Was this sombra Engaño? Maybe it was, maybe it wasn't. But there was only one way to find out. "Get out, Engaño!" I shouted.

The sombra looked surprised. I couldn't see its face, of course, but it lost its perfect, military-type stance; it staggered backwards a bit—looking this way and that, then over at Fuego. I couldn't be sure, but I thought I saw the hint of a smile hidden beneath Fuego's beard.

"Get out, I said!" I shouted again (hoping not to wake anyone up with all of my yelling). "You think I don't know who you are? You're Engaño! You're the same sombra that was here before trying to scare me! But I'm not scared of you!"

The arm holding the fireball dropped to its side.

"You have no right to be here!" I continued, hands clenched tightly at my sides. "You lost the right to hang around me the day I was adopted into the King's family! I'm the King's daughter now, so messing with me means messing with the King! So . . . I command you to leave . . . right now!"

The sombra was looking more nervous—and more vulnerable—by the second.

"*Leave!*" I shouted at the shadow. "In the name of the P—"

The next thing I knew, a ball of fire was flying directly at my face. The visor (which I had lifted in order to see better) fell down over my face a split-second before the fireball reached me; I was not touched. But the force of the blow itself crumbled me to the floor. Through the small holes in the visor, I could see Fuego; he was flying at the sombra—his long, silver sword penetrating the darkness. I watched the black shadow collapse onto the floor and fade. Engaño wouldn't be bothering me again.

I sat there for what seemed like forever, trying to clear

my head. The blow had hurt, but I was still able to think clearly enough to realize that the King had saved my life. I was certain that he had been the one to cause the visor to fall down over my face the second before the fireball hit. Otherwise I would have been toast.

"Thank you, Father," I whispered, still trying to catch my breath. "Thank you for saving me."

I thanked Fuego, too, but he didn't respond. I guess he felt as though he didn't deserve any praise; he was just doing his duty.

I decided I'd had enough reading for one night and headed for bed. I picked up the Book of Light from off the floor, closed it, and silently slid it beneath the bed. Then I thought better of it and pulled it back out. I opened it up and left it that way for the remainder of the night—open and bright for any passersby to observe.

CHAPTER 32

The Journal

W e went to the mall again. This time Dad and Uncle
Antonio went with us. I wondered how it would
work out. Would Dad just be negative the whole time and
spoil the trip? But at the same time I was thrilled; at least he
was finally wanting to do stuff with the family.

The mall was as crowded as I remembered—perhaps
more so. The criados were *everywhere*, and they were interesting to observe; there seemed to be all kinds. Some were
like Fuego—serious and silent, and yet more than ready to
jump into action at the slightest sign of a brawl. Others
were more like Mensajero—warm and friendly and quite
personable. In fact, some of the criados were so caught up
in conversation that they were nearly distracted from their
work. They had to be reminded by a tap on the shoulder or
a word from a fellow criado that their work was over here
and not to be talking so much. Fuego wasn't a big talker;
when he ran into a fellow worker that he knew he merely
gave a quick nod and maybe a smile. He and I were a lot
alike, really.

The mall was not void of sombras. There were a few

lurking here and there—usually in the shadows, and nearly always at a safe distance from the criados. There were some exceptions, of course; I noted a few particularly brazen sombras that were daring enough to walk out into the open among the criados. At one point, I watched as a sombra and a criado crossed paths. The criado immediately drew his sword while the sombra continued on—seemingly oblivious to the criado's presence. (I think they exchanged glances as they passed, though.) I didn't understand this. Why didn't the criado challenge it to a duel or attack the sombra as soon as its back was turned? (No, I suppose criados are too honorable for that sort of thing.) I decided that these daring sombras must have been there by *right*, somehow—that they had a right to be there for some reason I was unaware of. It might have had something to do with the humans they were with because, curiously, the sombras that were bold enough to make their way out into the open were never without a person nearby. Whatever the reason, I tried to keep my distance from these sombras as much as possible.

On our way to the food court, we passed by a video arcade. Video arcades are always dark (for some reason), but today it seemed darker than usual. I stopped to look: amid all the flashing lights and noisy games were sombras—moving to and fro around the room like a swarm of wasps. The dark shadows seemed to favor the violent video games best, for this was where they hung out most. The players of the games, of course, were completely unaware of the sombras standing over them.

"Let's go in there!" Jaime exclaimed, starting towards the dark room. I quickly took his hand and hurried him along.

When it was nearly time to go, we stopped by one last shop hidden away in a corner of the mall. (There were no sombras here.) They sold neat stuff like books and journals and bracelets. I liked it, but I noticed that my dad seemed to feel uncomfortable most of the time we were there. I looked at the journals. *Not* the diaries; diaries are for little girls with big brothers who might steal into her room and read what she's written and so it has to be protected with a lock and key. A journal has no lock; it's for older kids who don't need a lock and key because they know well how to hide secret things. I picked up one with different-colored shapes on the cover. I needed a place to write stuff other than on comic strips, and I knew of lots of good hiding places.

We got home around 4:30. After supper, I headed up to the treehouse to try out my new journal. (Jaime had gotten a new board game at the mall, so he was temporarily preoccupied.) I opened it up: blank lines covered the pages of the journal—surrounded by a border of colorful shapes. I thought about what to write. Some people write their feelings in journals. Some people write about experiences.

I tapped my pen against my chin in thought. Then I began to write:

I went to the mall today with Aunt Sarah. It was fun. We got to eat in the food court (there were a lot of criados in there!), and I bought this journal. Now I'm trying to decide what to write in it.

I tapped my pen against the treehouse floor. It sounded hollow.

Dad went with us. He did okay, I guess. He wasn't real happy-acting, or anything, but I've seen worse. (I've seen a lot worse.) He seems to be trying harder lately to be agreeable. Maybe it's because we're here at Uncle Antonio's house. When we go back home, he'll probably start being negative again.

I paused.

It really bothers me how Dad is always negative. I don't know why, either. I don't know why he's negative, I mean. It makes me not want to be around him. And –

I paused again.

And, the thing is, I <u>want</u> to be around him. I just—I just want him to like me.

I looked up at the sky to keep the tears that had welled up in my eyes from finding their way out. I saw Fuego watching me. He slowly began to climb down the tree towards me. (He could have flown, of course, but I guess he didn't feel like flying.) He dropped into the treehouse and, surprisingly, knelt down on the floor next to me on both knees. I looked at his face; tears were streaming down his cheeks and running into his beard. I watched as he gently reached over and touched my cheek—although of course I could not actually feel his hand on my face. Then he briefly abandoned his sword to embrace me in a criado hug—a hug that you can't feel but you know is there.

I felt better after that, but I also felt a little worried. How could Fuego afford to take such a risk? He had abandoned his post, his job of guarding me. A sombra could quite easily attack now—*both* of us were in danger. Who would watch over us now that Fuego was off duty?

I looked up and got my answer: sitting in the tree above us were *many* criados—all of them with swords drawn and all of them with looks on their faces that would warn any sombra that valued its life to keep its distance.

CHAPTER 33

The Noble Warrior

The next day was Sunday, and I slept late because I knew that the rest of the family (except for Dad, of course) would be gone when I got up. I could have my time alone to read the Book of Light then. (I was surprised to find myself almost wishing I had gone with them to church.)

I stayed in bed until 10:00—which is pretty late for someone who is used to getting up at the crack of dawn. Ten o'clock is that magical hour when bright things look even brighter and dark things are covered with light as the sun blazes out as if to say, "It's going to be a good day; everything will work out."

I got out of bed with a smile on my face. I even found myself trying to whistle (which was a talent I had never quite been able to master) as I entered the kitchen and fixed myself a bowl of cereal. Rats! We were out of Cap'n Crunch! I settled for Raisin Bran. I opened the refrigerator and got the milk out—pouring it onto the bran flakes and raisins. Then I opened the refrigerator door back, set the milk inside, and turned around. Dad was standing there.

I don't know why, but I jumped. I was holding my cereal

bowl, and some of the cereal spilled onto the floor. "Oh, hi Dad," I said.

He didn't say a word. He only stared at me.

Maybe he hadn't heard me. "Hi, Dad," I repeated.

What was that look on his face? Was he angry with me? Why was he staring at me like that? Besides looking bedraggled after having just woken up (his hair was a mess), he had a strange look in his eyes.

"Dad," I repeated, beginning to feel nervous. "Dad, what's the matter?"

Suddenly, I looked down: I was wearing my armor. I looked at my dad; he couldn't see it, could he? Surely he couldn't see it. He didn't have the Power of Paraíso. So what was he looking at? I looked down at my armor again. I looked up and shrieked—dropping my cereal bowl onto the floor. Standing directly behind my dad—with its claws digging into the top of his head—was a sombra.

I gasped and stumbled backwards—nearly slipping on the milk in my metal shoes. The sombra looked at me; I could almost see the evil grin on its dark face.

Suddenly, another shadow entered the room through the outside wall. It approached the first sombra; both sombras looked at each other then—realizing that the first sombra had its hands full—the second sombra started towards me.

Terrified, I backed into the corner—over by the sink. I was trapped, with no way out. The kitchen only had a narrow opening, and the sombra was blocking it. *I'm a warrior,* I repeated over and over in my mind. *I'm a warrior; I don't have to be afraid.* But the words weren't reaching my heart.

The sombra walked towards me with slow, deliberate steps. In two more steps it would reach me; I would be in the hands of a sombra—just like my dad. *I'm a warrior of the King—I don't have to be afraid—the thing can't hurt me.*

I felt helpless—like an animal being preyed upon that

knows its time is near. I had been about to have breakfast; now it was the creature's turn.

I braced myself on the counter behind me, closed my eyes tight, and awaited the inevitable. *Save me, Father!* I pleaded in my mind.

Suddenly, the sombra lunged towards me—about to dig its claws into my head. But I never felt a thing because a blinding light suddenly appeared from somewhere. I opened my eyes to see the dark shadow wringing its hands and shaking them violently as if it had just been badly burned. I looked at its hands: the creature's claws were gone—my protective helmet had burned them completely off! The sombra had tried to penetrate my head, but it could not get past my armor.

The sombra began to back away from me—I imagined a look of anger mixed with extreme horror on its face. I stood there breathing heavily—still gripping the counter behind me. But the fear was quickly leaving me.

I took a step towards the sombra. The creature was in the living room now—still shaking its now clawless hands in agony.

I continued towards it—slowly and steadily, like a warrior. I would be controlled by it no longer.

The sombra was so preoccupied with its clawless condition that it failed to notice me at first. When it did notice me, its reaction was unmistakable: one of sheer panic! It backed away from me—tripping and falling over its own feet (and wings). I continued on. The sombra got up and tried to stand but something knocked it back down to the floor again—I could almost hear the creature screech in anger. And I continued on.

It was madder than ever now—but it was also more *afraid* than ever; it knew its time was near. It had probably heard rumors of Engaño's fate.

I continued towards it, feeling more like a noble warrior

every second. "You have no power over me," I said to the dark shadow cowering in the corner. I spoke in a voice loud enough for the sombra to hear but hopefully soft enough that my dad would not. "I'm done with you," I said to it. "You can never make me afraid again."

The sombra believed me and trembled.

"I'm the King's daughter now," I continued. "I don't know your name, but I know who sent you: Mentiroso, the leader of the sombras. He doesn't scare me, though, and neither do you. The Book of Light says," and here, the sombra clapped its still throbbing hands over its ears, "'Submit yourselves, then, to the King. Resist Mentiroso, and he will flee from you.'"

The sombra momentarily forgot about its defenseless position and was about to come at me anyway, but I was ready with a second round of ammunition. "'For the King has not given us a spirit of fear and timidity,'" I quoted, "'but of power, love, and self-discipline.'"

The creature tried to get away, but I was just getting started. "'But the King watches over those who fear him, those who rely on his unfailing love.'"

The sombra abandoned its desire for revenge and just wanted out of there. But as long as it was still in the house, it was all mine. "'Do not fear anything except the almighty King. He alone is worthy. If you fear him, you need fear nothing else.' 'The King is my light and my salvation—so why should I be afraid? The King protects me from danger—so why should I tremble?'"

And then, to finish off the trembling sombra with one final round of ammunition I had stored away: "'Finally, be strong in the King and in his mighty power. Put on the full armor of the King so that you can take your stand against the enemy's schemes. For our struggle is not against flesh and blood, but against the rulers, against the authorities, against the powers of this dark world and against the spiritual forces of evil in the heavenly realms. Therefore put on the full armor of the King, so that when the day of evil comes, you may be able to stand your ground, and after you have done everything, to stand.'

"The next time you see me," I told the cowering creature, "I'll have a sword. Prepare yourself."

Fuego stepped forward. The long, silver sword at its throat was enough for the sombra; it left the house.

I turned around. My dad was still there—now sitting on one of the stools with his head in his hands, looking miserable.

His head was also in another's hands. But the sombra had seen its friend's plight and made the choice not to hang around. It released my dad from its grip and flew the coop.

Relieved to see my dad freed from the clutches of the enemy (and relieved to not have to fight a second sombra), I started towards him. He looked so incredibly alone. I now forgot all about the angry look he had given me earlier and felt—for the first time, I think—compassion for him.

I took a seat on the stool next to his. "Dad," I said to him quietly, watching my armor fade, "it's safe for us to talk now."

CHAPTER 34

The Conversation

It felt weird sitting there with my dad. I wanted him to talk to me—more than anything else in the world—and yet I *didn't* want him to, either. I was scared. We'd never really talked before (at least without getting in a fight), and I was afraid to try. It's always scary to try something new, even if it's a good thing. Like I pointed out earlier, sometimes we push away from us those things that, deep down, we really want the most.

We sat there in silence for several minutes. It seemed like an eternity, but I was determined to make my dad do the talking. I could start the conversation—that would be easy. But I wanted to see if he could do it.

"Sara," he finally said. His voice sounded weak and frail. I'd never heard him sound that way before. He paused, and I waited patiently for him to continue. "I've thought a lot about what you said," he told me, "—the other day, in the living room, about me not talking to you." He cleared his throat. I could tell that this was very difficult for him. I wished I knew why.

He sat there, not looking at me but instead down at his

hands. *Help him, Father*, I said in my mind. *Help him say what he needs to say.*

He sat there for probably an entire minute before continuing. "I—I've never been very good at..." His voice broke and I thought he was going to cry. I looked at his face. This was a dad I had never seen before. I liked what I was seeing.

He took a deep breath and let it out in a sigh. He turned and looked at me for the first time. His eyes looked gentle, new. "You know," he said with a sniff. "This conversation might go a lot smoother if we were riding on top of Bob and Big Thunder."

I looked at him, surprised. Bob and Big Thunder, of course, were two of Uncle Antonio's horses. Dad didn't even *like* to ride.

"I'll bet we could have them saddled up and go for a quick ride before the others get back. What do you say?"

What did I *say?*

"Yes!"

It was the *perfect* day for a ride; the sun was out and the sky was blue. The birds sang all around us, and Big Thunder's shifting rhythm beneath me as we rode along— my dad beside me on Bob (a chestnut almost as big as Big Thunder)—all told me that all was right with the world. It felt good to be back on a horse again—even if it wasn't a flying horse.

My dad must have felt it, too, because before we had gone half a mile, Dad opened up and began to talk. "Did I ever tell you," he said to me, "about the day you were born?"

No, I was pretty sure he hadn't.

"Your mom was so excited to have you, Sara; she'd wanted a little girl ever since *she* was a little girl. You were literally a dream come true for her."

"Really?" I said. I couldn't imagine being anyone's dream come true.

My dad nodded. "I can still remember the look on her

face," he recalled with a smile, "when she found out that you were a girl."

I smiled, but I couldn't help remembering her with sadness, too. "Dad?" I said quietly—not out of fear, for once, but out of respect. "Dad, do you ever miss Mom?"

He didn't answer. We continued on in silence for several minutes. One of the horses sighed. "Yes, Sara," he said softly. "I miss her a lot."

I waited for him to say more. When he didn't, I said, "Me, too. I…" I hesitated. I didn't want what I was about to say to be taken the wrong way. "I—I sometimes wish that she were still here." I looked over at my dad. I hoped that my saying this wouldn't offend him.

"I wish for that every day, Sara," he told me.

I didn't respond but waited for him to continue.

"Someone like your Mom is not easily forgotten. She was my Spanish rose, Sara—my flower in the desert." I had to force myself to keep from laughing. I had never heard my dad talk like that before. "She put out a beautiful fragrance that drew everyone to herself. Everywhere we would go, all would say, 'There goes Spanish rose.' Her aroma touched everyone around her. You can't forget someone like that. I guess all you can do is pick up and go on, but it's hard. Very, very hard."

I was taken aback. I'd never heard my dad say that much at one time before. It was like he was suddenly a totally different person. If he said nothing else today, I would be satisfied.

But he said more. "What was it she used to say? 'The truth will set you free.'"

I turned to look at my dad in amazement. That was a verse from the Book of Light! Had my mother read from the Book of Light before she died? I decided not to say anything but instead wait and see if it came out in the conversation.

My dad sighed. "'The truth will set you free,'" he

repeated. "I never believed it before. I always thought it was a hoax—a cover-up for something. I always thought that there must be *another* reason why your mother chose to believe in truth." He paused. Under his breath, I heard him utter the word, "Truth." I watched him shake his head. "What *is* truth?" I heard him say.

I looked down at my belt. I couldn't see it—which was a good thing; it meant there were no sombras around. But I imagined the distinct "T" that stood for truth engraved on the front of it.

"Truth is for people like your mother," my dad continued with a sigh, "not for people like me. Truth is too good for me."

"Maybe truth is for everybody," I ventured, "you just have to know where to look for it."

My dad looked over at me. He hadn't been smiling up to this point, but now he cracked a smile. "You're a lot like your mother, Sara," he said, smiling. "That sounded exactly like something she would have said."

"Really?" I asked.

He gave a quick nod and looked away. The horses continued on in a slow walk. Time seemed to drag by for eternity. "I don't know," he finally said with another sigh. "Maybe I *should* put you back in church."

I nearly fell off my horse; he had said the "c" word!

"That was where your mother learned about truth. Maybe that's the *only* place to find it. She was happiest there, I know that. She always came home with a big smile on her face—ready to tell me the newest piece of 'truth' she'd learned." Dad grinned at the memory. "She never had enough to say about what she was learning from that book...what did she call it? 'The Book of Light.'"

I had to force my legs to remain still so that they wouldn't involuntarily begin to beat against Big Thunder's sides—breaking him into a trot. "The Book of Light?" I exclaimed, attempting to keep from shouting. "Mom read from the Book of Light?"

"The *whole* thing, Sara—cover to cover. She believed it all."

I was so ecstatic I thought I would scream.

"Of course, *I* never read it. I was always 'too good' for it." He chuckled to himself. "I guess I see now which of us was the 'good' one."

"What was her favorite verse?" I blurted out. I had to know.

Dad looked at me, then looked up, trying to remember. "'For the King so loved the world,'" he quoted, "'that he gave his one and only Son, that whoever believes in him shall not perish but have eternal life.' I think that was it."

If Big Thunder had sprouted wings at that moment and took off into the sky, I wouldn't have been more overjoyed. "That *is* a good one," I replied, as calmly as I could manage.

CHAPTER 35

The Sword of Espíritu

Knowing my mother was a warrior changed my entire outlook on life. I would be the best warrior I could—work harder at it than I ever had before. I would now fight the sombras without even a *trace* of fear in my heart because I knew that was what my mother had done. I didn't know much about her life as a warrior, of course, but I knew enough to know that she *was* one. If Dad knew her favorite verse out of the Book of Light, then that meant that she had told it to him on more than one occasion; otherwise, my dad wouldn't still remember it. And, in my mind, only the *strongest* warriors went around quoting verses from the Book of Light.

I would be a noble warrior. I would be one for my mother. I would fight sombras just the way my mother did.

Just as soon as I received the sword of Espíritu.

And then finally I did. It happened one morning as I was reading the Book of Light up in the treehouse and I heard a noise down below. It was still dark outside (probably around 5:30; remember, I got up *early* to read the Book of Light!) and I cautiously stood up and looked over the treehouse wall to see what had made the noise. It was too dark; I couldn't see anything or anyone. Suddenly, I heard a rustle in the leaves just above my head. I looked up to see a monstrous black shadow lunging towards me. I couldn't get out of the way in time; it knocked me to the treehouse floor. I could feel its horrible presence holding me down. I reached for the Book of Light, but it was out of reach. I tried to push the creature off of me, but the sombra had a tight hold—pinning me to the floor.

But I wasn't afraid of the snarling shadow; I was wearing my protective armor. Its terrible head dove at my face—attempting to bite me. My helmet of salvation was on; it got a mouthful of metal.

This angered the sombra; it let its guard down for a moment—just long enough for me to seize the opportunity. I heaved the mighty creature off of me and again went for the Book of Light—still open, still emitting light. It caught my foot and I hit the floor with a bang. The wind would have been knocked out of me had my breastplate of righteousness not been in place. I reached down and tried to uncurl the taloned fingers from around my ankle, but its hold was too tight. I watched as its gaping mouth bit again and again at my foot, but—because of my shoes of peace—this felt more like a puppy dog gnawing on my foot than this wolf-like creature.

I reached again for the Book of Light—beginning to pull myself towards it. I was merely inches away when the creature leapt onto my back. My back was unprotected; I felt its razor-sharp talons digging into my flesh. I cried out and swung over—knocking the sombra into the treehouse wall.

Now was my chance! I grabbed the Book of Light and aimed the beam of light directly at the creature. The light hit it so hard that I thought it would blast the sombra completely through the wooden wall. The dark shadow screamed out in pain, like a cougar being burned by fire. I held it there—pinning it to the wall. The sombra tried desperately to wriggle out from under the light, but the Book of Light held fast.

Suddenly, the sombra began to fade. Yes! It was almost gone! All I had to do was hold the Book of Light steadily at the darkness and eventually the powerful light would burn it away!

Seeing that it was fading, the sombra let out a howl and tried to move. It seemed that every ounce of energy was required of it; the Book of Light was draining it of its power. The sombra gave up and went limp. It immediately began trying again—attempting to lift its arms. What was it doing? It appeared to be making something with its hands.

The shadow was almost completely gone now. What was that in its hand?

In one final burst of energy the sombra lifted one of its arms and directed a fireball straight at my head. I was not prepared for this like I should have been. Had I anticipated this maneuver, I could have been holding the Book of Light with one hand while using shield of faith with the other to shield me from the sombra's fiery dart. The ball of fire would have deflected off the shield and the sombra would have soon after faded away completely.

But I was not prepared; the fireball hit me head-on and knocked me to the floor—sending the Book of Light sailing across the treehouse and landing in an upside-down position in the corner.

The sombra wasted no time and flew at me. In half a second it was on top of me; I could feel its hot breath through my visor. The fire had not touched me because of my helmet of salvation, but I had fallen so hard against the treehouse wall that it took me a moment to clear my head. *I have to get at the Book of Light,* I thought to myself. *It's my only weapon.* I was no match for the sombra's strength without the Book of Light.

Then suddenly I remembered: I *did* have the Book of Light...

"'Submit yourselves, then,'" I struggled to say—the creature's massive weight heavy upon me.

The creature opened its gaping mouth and roared in my face—showing me its fangs.

But I would *not* be intimidated. "'Submit yourselves, then,'" I quoted, louder this time, "to the *King!* Resist Mentiroso, and he will *flee from you!*"

The sombra roared again and attempted to roll me over so that it could get at my back—my one place of vulnerability. It accidentally rolled me too hard and I ended up in the corner of the treehouse—the corner with the Book of Light! I grabbed it up and nearly had it aimed at the sombra when the Book was suddenly knocked from my hands and went flying over the treehouse wall. I watched it fall; a yellow ball of fire trailed closely behind it.

Now what? I looked around for some other weapon I could use. There *was* no other weapon, and the sombra knew it, too. I could almost see its evil eyes laughing at me. I was cornered with no way out.

I didn't feel like a warrior anymore. I felt like a victim. Slowly, I slid down to the floor—my back to the wall. I felt tears beginning to fill my eyes.

The sombra looked at me and laughed. It got down on all fours and walked from one side of the treehouse to the other—like a lion that had discovered its prey and was merely waiting for the right moment at which to spring.

I didn't care anymore. I had lost. Who was I kidding? I was no match for this creature. Besides, I was tired. I didn't have any strength left with which to fight.

Suddenly, a verse flooded my mind as brightly as the Book of Light itself:

"Don't be afraid, for I am with you. Do not be dismayed, for I am your King. I will strengthen you. I will help

you. I will uphold you with my victorious right hand."

"Oh, King," I cried out with my remaining strength, "I don't have enough strength left to overcome this evil. Please help me."

The sombra saw and heard me talking to the King, and it wasted no more time: it sprung at me. Suddenly, there was a blinding light and the creature fell over backwards, screeching. It now cowered in the opposite corner—breathing heavily like an animal that had just been cheated out of its next meal.

I didn't know what had just happened, but the bright light seemed to have had a strange effect on me; I could feel my strength returning.

Slowly, I rose to my feet. As I stood up, I felt my left hand brush against something hard. I looked down: The sword of Espíritu had arrived and was in its sheath!

My attention was instantly directed toward the sombra as it swiftly took to the air. It hovered higher and higher—its giant wings flapping—into the highest branch it could find. Then, with all the strength it could muster, it dove straight towards me.

But my sword came between us. It was presently unsheathed and piercing the darkness—right through its center.

The sombra staggered, fell, and faded. I had won.

Or rather, the King had. As I sheathed my newest piece of armor, I praised my Father the King for his faithfulness. He had saved me once again.

As I climbed down the treehouse ladder by the newly-rising sun, I found the Book of Light where it had fallen. I brushed it off, sheathed it under my arm, and headed inside.

CHAPTER 36

Sword Practice

The sword of Espíritu. It was a beauty. Laid over in pure gold, the hilt reflected the sun's rays in almost a blinding light. Embedded in the gold on both sides of the hilt were two rubies—positioned in such a way that they reminded me of Espíritu's fiery red eyes. And engraved into the cross section of the hilt, where the vertical and horizontal parts met, was a single letter: the letter "E."

My armor was finally complete. I had all I needed now to win a fight against Mentiroso.

But was I ready? I wasn't sure. After all, from what I had heard and read about him, Mentiroso was no ordinary sombra. He would certainly not allow himself to be killed as easily and as quickly as the sombras that had gone before him. He was far too shrewd for that.

As I examined the sword of Espíritu while sitting on Jaime's bed, I wondered if I had what it took. The sword was powerful enough—I knew that already. Only one look at it was required to realize this: The silver blade was long, thick, and had a double edge. Most importantly, of course, I knew that it was empowered by the King himself.

"It seems almost a shame that it has to be used as a weapon," I thought aloud. "It's far too sacred an object to actually *use*."

I swung it around a couple times. Like the shield, it was just the right weight for me: not too heavy, but not too light, either. I wondered if I should practice with it. The rest of the family had gone to the store; I would have a few minutes to myself.

I stood to my feet. Now, let's see—what did I remember from the movies? How does one fight with a sword? I tried the basic forward motion, called a "thrust." That was easy enough. But what if a sombra snuck up on me from behind? I spun around and pretended to slash a sombra in half—holding onto the sword with only my right hand. A loud clang ensued as the sword's blade came into contact with a leg of the bed. The noise startled me so badly that I dropped the sword. "Oops," I said, picking it up. I observed the damage. Thank goodness it had been the flat side of the blade that had hit. Jaime would have been sleeping on a three-legged bed otherwise. I would have to be more careful with this thing; it was certainly sharp enough to do some major damage to this room.

I decided that I had lost control of the sword because it was too heavy to be swung around with only one hand. I tried it again (stepping back a little ways from the bed), this time holding the hilt with both hands. I found myself better able to control it. Using both hands, I swung the sword to the right. Then to the left. I tried another forward thrust motion. Unfortunately, I underestimated the length of the sword and pierced the wall with the blade. "Oh, great," I said, attempting to pull the sword out of the wall. It was stuck in there pretty far—about a foot of the sword was missing. I pulled on the hilt with both hands, but the sword's blade held fast. "Come on!" I said, arguing with it. "I can't have a sword stuck in the wall when Aunt Sarah and Uncle

Antonio get home! Get out of there!" I pulled with all my might. Finally, the sword came loose. Again, I examined the damage. There was a three-inch hole in the wall. I didn't figure anyone would notice.

Just to be sure, though, I decided that Jaime's desk would look much better sitting in that spot as opposed to its present location. I shoved it over. There. That looked *much* better.

Now, back to sword practice. Thanks to my little accident, I knew how potentially dangerous my newfound hobby was. "Maybe I should take it outside," I decided. "Sword fighting is more of an *outdoor* sport, I think."

I went out into the backyard. There wasn't much out here; it wasn't much of a backyard at all, really. Only Uncle Antonio's grill that he used to fix burgers on, a couple of trees, and an old swing set that Jaime rarely, if ever, used.

I looked for a place to try out my sword. The swing set caught my eye. I walked over to it. Like all swing sets, it was made out of metal. *Surely this thing won't cut through metal,* I thought to myself.

I stepped back and positioned myself for a fight. I imagined that the pole of the swing set was the enemy. "Yaaaaww!" I cried, swinging the sword with all my might. I must have swung a little too hard because the bottom part of the pole was severed as easily as cutting paper.

"Oh, drat!" I yelled, stepping back out of the way as the swing set suddenly lurched forward. "Aunt Sarah's going to kill me!"

I looked at the swing set. It was teetering in a lopsided position. There was no way Jaime would be doing any swinging on it for *sure* now. Unless...

I walked around it. Wasn't it really too big for Jaime anyway? What if I helped him out by lowering it a little closer to the ground?

I checked out the severed piece of metal lying on the ground. It was about a foot long. I walked over to the pole diagonal from the first. I decided I couldn't leave the swing set lopsided; I'd better even it out a bit. Positioning myself for attack, I took a swipe at the pole at about a foot from the ground. In one swift move, the bottom portion of the pole was detached.

Now two of the poles were the length they were when I first got out there, and two of the poles were approximately a foot shorter. I couldn't leave it like this. I decided I'd better even it out all the way.

So that's what I did—taking swipes at the other two legs of the swing set until all four were perfectly even. "There," I announced proudly, inspecting my work. The fact of the matter was that the swing set would have been *perfect* for a child around the age of four or five. Too bad Jaime wasn't a child around the age of four or five.

Just then, I heard Aunt Sarah's Suburban pull up. Should I hide my sword? Aunt Sarah, being a warrior herself, had probably seen one before. But what about the others?

Jaime presently burst through the gate of the chain-link fence. "Sara," he called to me. "Mom says for you to come and help with the groceries." He didn't react to the sword in my hand. Naturally, he couldn't see it.

"Okay," I responded, sheathing the sword of Espíritu.

"Hey," he exclaimed, his big blue eyes getting even bigger. "What happened to my swing set?"

"What do you mean?" I asked, playing dumb.

"It…" Jaime was unsure now. "Didn't it used to be taller?"

I looked it over carefully. "I don't think so," I responded. "You sure you're feeling all right, Jaime? Maybe you're coming down with something." I paused for effect. "It *could* even be swordatoryitis!"

Jaime gasped and felt of his forehead. "Really?" he asked worriedly.

"Yeah," I nodded. "You might want to have Aunt Sarah take your temperature."

I started for the garage and the groceries. "Oh, and by the way," I added, turning towards him. "When you go in your room, don't be surprised if things look out of place. That's another symptom of the illness."

CHAPTER 37

The Black Hole

Sunday was fast approaching. So was the end of the summer. I decided to go to church with Aunt Sarah and Uncle Antonio. It could be my last chance.

I talked to the King about getting my Dad to go. I wanted him to go with me—more than anything else in the world—and I thought that there might be the slightest chance that he'd say yes. When the time came for me to ask him, he said that he'd think about it. Naturally, I was elated. Maybe my Dad had changed.

But when Sunday rolled around, I was met with bitter disappointment when—even though everyone else was ready to go—my Dad was still in bed. He had slept in again. Aunt Sarah said not to wake him. I argued with her, trying to explain to her that Dad really *did* want to go and that he would be disappointed if he woke up and found that we had left without him. Aunt Sarah told me that I couldn't change him, and that forcing my Dad to go to church wouldn't change anything if he "wasn't ready." I argued with her for a full ten minutes, but it was no use; I knew Aunt Sarah was right.

When we arrived at the church, I was shocked to see that it was the very church at which I had received the Book of Light! We walked down the main entrance hallway (with the lights turned *on* this time!) and through the double doors of the sanctuary. What a sight! Besides the room being filled with light, it was filled to the brim with criados—from top to bottom. I had never seen so many criados in one place before—not even at the mall! The mighty men with wings and swords seemed to have assumed one of three positions: either standing in the aisles beside the ones they guarded, hovering over them near the ceiling, or actually sitting in the pews with them! The pastor would be preaching to a larger audience this morning than he realized.

As the pastor approached the podium, I was again amazed to see that he was accompanied—not by one, but *four* criados! As he spoke, one criado stood to his left, one stood to his right, one stood behind him, and one hovered above him. *That should give him protection enough,* I thought to myself.

First came the music. This was my favorite part of the whole "church experience" because of what I heard. My Father allowed me for a brief time to be able to hear the voices of the criados. It was the most beautiful sound I had ever heard before or would ever hear again. Perhaps you've had the privilege of hearing a men's choir. It was like that, only better. The harmonies were *perfect*; not one of the criados sang off key, not one of them missed a note. It was like listening to "The Carol of the Bells"—only with voices instead of bells. Simply spectacular.

I was disappointed when the singing ended. Why did the criados stop singing? After all, the music director was still leading the music and the people in the congregation were still singing. But for some of the songs, the criados went silent. I don't think it was because they *couldn't* sing the songs; these winged men could probably hit any note of any musical scale in existence. I think it was that certain songs simply didn't pertain to them.

The sermon was about love—from the "love chapter" that Aunt Sarah (and maybe Mom) liked so much. It inspired me to want to love more. I wasn't very skilled at loving.

When the sermon was over, the pastor gave an invitation. I remembered vaguely what this was from my past experiences of church. This was when the pastor asked if anyone would like to "come forward" (come up to the front) to make a decision. I'd already "made a decision," so I wasn't sure why Espíritu was nudging me to go. I tried to ignore him. There were a lot of people in here; he probably just had the wrong person.

"Sara, do you want to go up there?" I heard a voice say to my right.

It was Aunt Sarah. How did she know?

I went. I'm still not sure why. Maybe I felt like I had to please Aunt Sarah. Maybe I knew that Espíritu would give me no rest until I did. Or maybe, just maybe, I did it because I *wanted* to—because I knew deep down that it was the right thing to do.

When we got home, the first thing I wanted to do was to tell Dad all about my experience. Aunt Sarah knew this and asked Jaime if he would like to go out for ice cream; his response was predictable. Uncle Antonio understood and went with them.

Left alone with Dad, I silently entered the living room— talking to the King as I went. I asked him to give me the words to say and the way to say them. I didn't want to mess things up like I usually did.

I took a seat on the couch. Dad was in his usual place in front of the TV. For once, though, it was turned off! It was a modern-day miracle.

I wasn't sure where to begin. All I knew was that I

wanted to remind my Dad what church was like. I wanted him to remember.

"Dad?"

He didn't respond but continued to stare straight ahead. I expected this. Even though he was starting to smile and talk to me more, the fact that I went to church this morning probably changed all that.

It *was* strange, however, how he continued to stare at a blank screen. It was as though he were going to extra lengths to ignore me this time.

"Dad, can I talk to you for a minute?"

"I'm in the middle of a program, Sara," he responded shortly.

I looked at the TV. What program? Oh, he must have meant a *radio* program. I noticed for the first time the sound of a radio turned on. He was probably catching the scores of a game.

I sighed. Television, radio—it was all the same: a distraction.

I curled up on the couch, staring blankly at the screen along with my Dad. It was incredible; he was so used to staring at a TV screen that he did it even when the TV was turned off.

"Well, when will it be…"

But I didn't finish. I had looked over at my Dad and saw something that sent chills up my spine. There, in the middle of the room, was what appeared to be a black hole; everything else in the room looked normal, but it was as though someone had taken a pair of scissors and cut a gaping hole out of this part of the room. Then I knew what was causing it: Sombras were crowding around my Dad so densely that all I could see was darkness.

I did then the bravest and craziest thing I had ever done: Drawing my sword (for it was now within reach), I leapt off the couch and ran straight into the crowd of sombras—slashing left and right. Several fell to the ground and faded. The rest of them flew in all directions—stopping a safe distance away like a flock of buzzards waiting to return to their meal as soon as I was gone.

But I wasn't going anywhere. "Dad, can I sit with you?" I asked, taking a seat on the arm of the easy chair without waiting for a response.

Dad looked at me strangely, then sighed. "I guess this show *is* a little too old for you," he said, pushing the power button on the remote. I watched in amazement as the TV screen changed colors—from pitch black to more of a grayish color. What had just happened?

Then I knew: The TV *had* been turned on, and my Dad had been watching a TV program, but there had been so many sombras on the set during the making of the movie that the actors were no longer visible. I had been watching another black hole.

"Dad," I said in a trembling voice, wiping a sweaty palm on the arm of the chair, "we really need to talk."

CHAPTER 38

Spanish Rose

M y sword remained unsheathed. I kept it out—just in case the sombras dared to get too close.

I was still sitting there with my Dad wondering how to begin when he shocked me by being the one to initiate the conversation. "I decided a long time ago, Sara," he said to me, "that what matters in life is not what you have or what you know—but what you *do* with what you have and what you know."

I held my breath, waiting for him to continue.

"Have I ever told you, Sara, the story of how your mother and I met?"

"I don't think so, Dad," I responded carefully. I knew he hadn't.

He took a deep breath, gathering his thoughts—and his courage. "As you know," he began, "I was born in México, along with your Uncle Antonio." (He had said "Mexico" the way the Spanish do—where the "x" sounds like an "h.") "México is a festive place…with fiestas and piñatas and buena comida." (That meant "good food"—I'd heard my Dad use that phrase on more than one occasion.) "Mexicanos" (or

"Mexicans") *"love* to celebrate, Sara, with bright colors and flavorful music. And they like to dance."

I thought I could hear my Dad smile. I tried to imagine my Dad dancing. It was hard to imagine.

I didn't know a lot about Mexico, of course; I'd always tried to pretend that Mexico wasn't a part of my heritage. But I knew enough about it to know that it was a festive place. One time at school, my class had celebrated Cinco de Mayo. There was music and bright colors and even a piñata! We got to break it open right there in the classroom! One boy (who was *proud* of his Mexican heritage) had brought some authentic Mexican food for us to eat. I had to admit that it was really good.

"I'm sure you already knew all that," my Dad continued, "but there may be a part of México that you are unfamiliar with. In addition to being a festive place full of fiestas and good times, México is also a very *poor* place, Sara. Half of the country's people live in poverty. That means that 50 million Mexicanos don't have enough food to eat or clothing to wear. *These* people of México do not celebrate, Sara. They starve. Many of them bring home less than $13 a week; that's $52 a month."

I thought about it. Fifty-two dollars a month wasn't a lot of money. I could easily spend $52 a *week* on fast food and clothes.

"When you're poor, Sara," he continued, "you have to make a living any way you can. You will sell anything you can in order to earn a little extra money. Some people in México sell candy. Others sell gum. And they don't live in houses like we do; they live in cardboard boxes, Sara, or under bridges—wherever they can find to escape from the wind and rain."

My Dad paused. I waited in silence for him to continue.

"No one *wants* to live this way, Sara," he said. "No one *chooses* to be poor. Every day, hundreds of Mexicanos come to America to try and escape a life of poverty. They want to start a new life and make things better for themselves. They don't want to leave their native country…it's their homeland, Sara—a part of who they are. But they don't want to starve, either." For a moment my Dad was silent. "I was one of those people, Sara."

"You were poor?" I asked.

"*Very* poor," he nodded. "My family couldn't even afford a simple meal for supper much of the time. We had to make do many times with only one meal a day, and sometimes less than that. Many times I felt as though there was no hope for my future, Sara. I was born into poverty, and I would die in poverty—and there seemed to be nothing I could do to change it."

He paused. It almost seemed he wanted to add extra significance to what he was about to say. "Then your mother came into my life," he said. I thought I heard his voice crack.

"Go on," I urged gently.

"Well," he said, "your mother was not like me, Sara—in many ways. She was not as poor as I. She could afford things like decent clothing and enough food. I envied her, to tell you the truth. I would often see her out selling flowers on the street corner. Only the 'wealthy' (or wealthier than us) sold flowers, Sara, because flowers were expensive. If you could afford to buy and sell flowers, then that meant that you lived a pretty decent life—or at least had enough money to eat more than one meal a day.

"But there was an even bigger difference between me and your mother than how much money we had. Your mother had something that I wanted even more than money."

He paused, leaving me in suspense. "What?" I asked.

When he finally responded, my Dad's voice sounded far away. "Joy," he said. "Your mother was nearly always either smiling or laughing, Sara." I could tell that my Dad was smiling for sure now. "Our 'house,'" he continued, "was located near a small church on the edge of town. Of course, my family never went because we were too poor; we didn't own clothing decent enough to enter a church building (or so we thought). But, because we lived nearby, we saw every Sunday the people going in and out. I always wondered what went on in there, Sara.

"Well, your mother would oftentimes choose the outside of that church as a place to sell her flowers. On one particular Sunday, your mother (she was about your age at the time, maybe a little older) was there selling her flowers like usual. She was probably hoping that these people wealthy enough to go to church on Sunday would have enough money to buy a flower from her. She was selling roses that day—the most expensive flowers one could buy. She was as beautiful, Sara, as the roses she held in her hand. Her long, black hair blowing in the wind, her black eyes, her kind smile." I heard my Dad remembering. "She was still dirty; it was impossible to remain clean with the dirt from the streets always blowing in your face. But she was beautiful nonetheless. And the aroma she gave off to every person who passed her by was just as fragrant. She had something more than flowers to offer the people, Sara; she had kindness and joy."

My Dad took a deep breath. "Well, I had to see her, Sara. I just *had* to…I mean, up close. She was too beautiful for me not to. So I hurried over to where she was and hid behind a tree. I tried not to make a noise, but some of the local dirt got in my mouth and I coughed. She turned around. Our eyes met. I'll never forget the way she looked at me; she wasn't enamored, and she wasn't repulsed. In fact, it was difficult for me to understand exactly *what* she was thinking.

"Then, to my surprise, she reached out her hand. She was offering me a rose. She wasn't offering it to me to *buy*, Sara; she was offering it to me as a *gift*. I had never seen such generosity. This was her livelihood—this was how she and her family made a living. And yet she saw my extreme poverty and offered me a rose for *free.*

"I didn't take it. Oh, how I wished I had—but I was much too afraid. I had never been offered a free gift before. I figured she would expect something in return, and I had nothing to offer."

Dad paused a moment to re-gather his thoughts. "Well, eventually we *did* meet. We became best friends and did everything together. When we were older, I asked her to marry me. We were both still poor, so we decided to come to America where the opportunities would be greater. Your Uncle Antonio came with us. It was here that he met your Aunt Sarah. They, too, fell in love and were married. Your mother was very fond of your Aunt Sarah, Sara; they immediately became the best of friends. They went shopping together, talked together…you know, did things that girls do."

I smiled. My Dad knew I wasn't a "typical" girl.

"Aunt Sarah shared with your mother about the Book of Light, and your mother became a believer. I never bought into it, of course, but—I can tell you this, Sara: I *did* notice a change in your mother after that. She was always kind and generous before, but now she had a *reason* to be kind and generous. Church became her life; to her, the Book of Light was 'the greatest treasure in the world.' She vowed to Aunt Sarah that—if she ever had a girl—she would name the child after her. Guess what?" he said, giving me the slightest squeeze. "She had a girl."

I slid down the arm of the chair into my Daddy's lap. For once, I felt safe in his arms. "Thanks for telling me, Dad," I whispered.

CHAPTER 39

Scattering Shadows

B arriers were broken that afternoon. Not only had I faced multiple sombras without fear, but I felt that Dad had revealed his heart to me for the first time ever. This barrier was an even more important one to me than the sombras.

But I'm afraid that I allowed the part about the sombras go to my head. I got a little cocky after that—thinking that I could defeat them without any help from others… *including* the King. I neglected Fuego's warning to never try fighting a sombra by my own power. I slashed through sombras left and right on many occasions—leaving none alive. It was easy for me. I wasn't afraid. But sometimes those things which are easy for us can cause us to become lazy.

I found this out the hard way. I was reading a book one afternoon (*not* the Book of Light, I might add) on the couch in the living room. Suddenly, I felt that I was not alone. I looked up; several sombras were approaching. I thought nothing of it and went back to my book. Several minutes later, I looked up; more sombras were there than before. Still I ignored them and continued to read. When I looked up for the third time, I was completely surrounded on every side by sombras. They had encircled me—transforming the couch I was sitting on into an island surrounded by dark waters.

I decided now would be a good time to take action. I laid down my book and stood to my feet—only feet away from the closest shadows. "I'm not sure why you're here," I said calmly to the sombra standing nearest to me. "You know how dangerous I am with a sword. Do you not fear for your lives?" I asked them all, looking around at the shadows. "Do you not worry that you will be cut to smithereens? So be it."

I reached for my sword. I fumbled for the hilt. I didn't feel it. I looked down.

My sword was gone!

Panic flooded my heart. I looked up: The sombras were beginning to move in closer.

"Fuego! Fuego, where are you?" I cried out in desperation.

There was no response.

I looked for an opening—a hole in the circle of shadows. There was none. The few that existed were quickly closing up; new sombras were arriving to fill them in.

I began to walk...and stumbled. I tried to get to my feet. I was knocked back down to the floor. I still had my shield! I covered myself with it; it was large enough to shield my entire body—especially now that I was curled up into a tight little ball on the floor. I wasn't expecting ammunition; an especially large fireball blasted the shield from my arm.

I crouched on the floor on all fours, panting like a cornered animal. I looked up at the monsters...so real...so close...so dark. What protection had I now? Sure, I still had the rest of my armor, but how long would it last? Without my sword, I was utterly defenseless.

In sheer defeat, I lifted up my head and hands. "Save me, King," I pleaded.

As I watched, the sombras—standing stock still up till now—suddenly began to shift and quake. They seemed restless, as though some outside force were causing them to lose confidence.

What happened next is hard to explain: Have you ever seen a pond or a stream teeming with tadpoles? If you touch the water, you will observe a moment of mass confusion as the tadpoles scatter in every direction away from your finger. That's how it was for me now: someone had "touched the water," and the "tadpoles" were scattering.

My first thought was that Fuego had arrived—scaring them off. So when I uncovered my face and opened my eyes, I was surprised to see Aunt Sarah walking towards me.

"Aunt Sarah!" I cried, stumbling to my feet. I threw myself at her in an embrace. "Aunt Sarah, you saved me!"

"The *Prince* saved you," she corrected me. "What's wrong, Sara?"

"It was horrible!" I exclaimed. "Like a bad dream."

"Well, it's over now," she reassured me, stroking my hair.

For a moment I was silent. Then I looked up into Aunt Sarah's beautiful blue eyes. "Aunt Sarah," I said to her, "how do you do it?"

"How do I do what?" she asked.

"How do you scare sombras so easily?"

"Sombras are naturally afraid of warriors, Sara," she responded.

"They weren't afraid of *me*."

Aunt Sarah paused, as though seeking guidance as to what to say. "Where's your sword?" she asked me.

"What?" I asked, shocked.

"Where's your sword?" she repeated.

My armor had disappeared along with the sombras. How did Aunt Sarah know I was missing my sword? Was Espíritu telling on me again? "I—I don't have it anymore," I confessed. "How did you know?"

Again, she was silent. "Sara, come sit down," she finally said, leading me to the couch. "You know, Sara," she told me. "Your sword is only as good as your Book—and I'm not talking about this one." She held up the book I had been reading. "I'm talking about the Book of Light."

"I've still got it," I assured her. "It's in there under Jaime's bed."

"That's exactly my point," Aunt Sarah responded. "When was the last time you read from it, Sara?"

I had been hoping she wouldn't ask that question. Typically, I was very good about remembering to read from the Book of Light every day—like every warrior should. Lately, however, I'd slacked off a bit—but I hadn't thought anyone knew about it. Aunt Sarah always seemed to have a way of knowing things.

"It's simple," she explained. "You lost your sword, Sara, because you lost the Word. They're one and the same. You can't have one without the other."

"Will I ever get it back?" I asked worriedly.

"Yes, you can get it back," she answered, "but it will take time—just like it took time to lose it. A weapon requires upkeep; you must sacrifice your time and effort to keep it sharp. If it goes dull, then you must work to make it sharp again. An unsharpened sword is a useless sword."

I spent time the following morning sharpening my sword. And the day after that. And the day after that. I pulled out the Book of Light, dusted it off, and opened it. The light stung my eyes at first for lack of use, but I didn't even mind. I determined I would get my sword back—whatever it took—and, once I had it, to never allow it to become dull again.

CHAPTER 40

Extra Help

E very morning after that, right after getting out of bed (and telling the King "good morning"), I would kneel down and ask the King to place his armor on me—just for that day. I asked him to "suit me up" and to send his criados to protect me. I recognized that the armor I owned wasn't mine at all but the King's, and that I should be requesting it rather than expecting it. I didn't ask for yearly armor or even weekly armor, but *daily* armor. My sombra problems would be enough for that day.

The King answered my requests and renewed my armor every morning. But I still didn't have a sword. It would be up to me to regain *that* piece.

I quickly discovered the perils of living life without a sword. I found that I was forced to work *twice* as hard in battle as I should have had to. And, on many occasions, all I could do was hide. It was a terrible blow for a practiced warrior to have to hide, but what else could I do? I had no offensive weapon with which to fight.

"Get back!" I yelled one day as two different sombras were getting too close. "I said get *back!*"

Of course they didn't listen but continued to advance. One thing about sombras is that they have a *major* problem with obedience.

"Get back! In the name of—"

They must have *really* not wanted to hear the name because two fireballs came spinning my way. I ducked quickly behind the kitchen table just in time to watch them bounce off and leave two oversized burnt spots on the wooden surface. Where's a tablecloth when you need one?

I made a break for it and took off in the direction of Uncle Antonio's easy chair. I jumped behind it as another fiery dart flew past my head. Why did I feel like I was in the middle of a war zone? Maybe because I *was* in the middle of a war zone.

I picked up the closest thing to me (which just happened to be the TV remote) and threw it. It passed right through the shadow. *Okay, Sara, that was really smart. It's just a shadow—what did you expect?*

Okay, so...how was I going to get out of this? I considered fleeing out the front door, then reconsidered this maneuver: sombras have wings; they'd more than likely catch up with me.

"Prince of Paraíso, please help me," I said. "Protect me with your mighty criados."

"Yaaaaaaww!"

I spun around; Fuego had stepped out from behind me and was charging—sword outstretched.

"You think you can mess with Paraíso's princess *that* easily, eh? We'll just see about that! Yaaaaaaaaww!"

I watched as Fuego brought his sword down as hard as he could on one of the sombras. It moved away just in time and escaped.

"Stand still and fight, you yellow-livered shadow! I never thought a black shadow could be so yellow! Ha!"

It wasn't a very clever joke, but Fuego must have

thought so.

"Hey, where do you think you're going, slimy scum? Come back and have a taste of my sword! Retreating into the kitchen now, eh? That's the *perfect* place to give you a proper taste! Come on out here and fight, you shady-suited grease bag!"

Up till now I had been so caught up in the fight that it hadn't even occurred to me that the King was allowing me to hear Fuego speak!

"Is that the best you can do? Yield me your best or else I shall grow bored and fall asleep, you scaly-skinned bat-brain!"

Fuego missed again; the sombra sent him sprawling to the floor. "Ow," he mumbled.

There was suddenly a flutter of wings as a bright light rushed into the room. It was Mensajero!

"No help needed," Fuego called out to him from the floor. "I've got this one perfectly under control, thank you."

"So I see," Mensajero said, already beginning to fight. "And I suppose you have that one perfectly under control, as well?" he said, referring to the second sombra.

"I was getting to that one," Fuego responded, getting to his feet. "Now, if you'll excuse me, I'll get back to my business now..."

"*Your* business is with the little one," Mensajero stated firmly, indicating me with his sword. "Stand near her and see that she comes to no harm."

"Oh, horse feathers!" Fuego grumbled, dusting himself off. "I *never* get to have any fun while *you're* around!" Begrudgingly, Fuego started towards me. But the other sombra was following him and gave him a good excuse to turn around and fight. "Sorry, Mensa, my man," Fuego chortled, "but duty calls!"

"Stay near the girl," Mensajero reiterated forcefully.

"All right, all right—don't get your lovely feathers all

ruffled up," Fuego grumbled, backing towards me (while continuing to fight). I heard him mumble under his breath, "*This* one's more difficult anyway."

"I heard that," called Mensajero.

"It's not fair that I get stuck with Miedo and you get to have it out with Orgullo," Fuego complained, continuing to guard me. "Orgullo is more in my league."

"Keep your eyes on the danger in front of you, Fuego," Mensajero ordered the subordinate criado.

Fuego obeyed, but I heard him mutter under his breath, "Hardly any danger at all."

Both criados continued to fight for my safety—keeping the sombras at bay. Suddenly, I looked down: *The sword of Espíritu was in my hand!*

I immediately stepped out from behind the easy chair and joined in the fight. When Fuego saw me, he laughed out loud—a great bellowing laugh. "Mensa, my man, look at this!" he called out. "We've got extra help!"

Mensajero turned briefly away from the sombra that presently held his attention. "Sara!" he exclaimed, seeing me. "What are you doing?" Then he remembered that I was a warrior and quickly rethought the matter. "I mean, are you *sure*, little one?" he asked in a more considerate tone. "Sombras are not for the working upon by one such as yourself."

In one swift movement, I thrust my sword into the sombra (apparently the one called "Miedo")—falling it to the floor. The shadow quickly faded. "Maybe not," I said, turning to face the head criado, "but sombras *are* for the working upon by the *King*, and the King works through me."

Both criados looked at each other.

"She was assigned to *me*," Fuego boasted.

CHAPTER 41

Mentiroso

My summer vacation was nearly over; I would leave tomorrow to go back home. I was surprised to find myself actually a bit disappointed. School would be starting soon; of course I wasn't looking forward to that. (But it *would* be kind of cool, I decided, to be escorted to class by my own personal bodyguard!)

I was starting to notice a difference in my Dad. I think he was smiling more than he used to—and was even watching television less! (This may have had something to do with the fact that I'd broken the remote.) When I told Dad I'd like to take a trip to Mexico some day, he didn't even mention about money. In fact, he said we could take a plane!

I was noticing a change in myself, as well. Aunt Sarah was no longer merely my aunt; she was my mentor and my friend. I no longer despised the light I saw in her eyes. In fact, I was beginning to think that—whenever I looked in the mirror—a similar light was shining in my own eyes. Maybe once the light from the Book of Light gets in your eyes it has trouble coming out.

Jaime was even different. When I pulled the Book of Light out from under Jaime's bed that day, I noticed a change in its appearance: at least a dozen comic strips were hanging out. I smiled. Someone besides me had been reading it.

Jaime walked into the room and saw me holding it.

"Nice bookmarks," I grinned.

He returned the grin with that big, beautiful smile of his.

I would miss Jaime. Maybe we could write.

There was one last thing I had to do before I left. After supper was over and I'd helped clear off the table and wash off the tablecloth (Aunt Sarah had bought a tablecloth to cover the two "mystery" burnt spots), I headed out to the barn to pay the horses one last visit.

The sky was growing dark. The time was about 7:00 in the evening, so the shadows were getting long as the sun hung low in the sky. Aunt Sarah didn't like me out at the barn after dark—it would have to be a short visit.

As I started for the barn, I suddenly noticed that I couldn't feel the dirt road beneath my feet. I looked down: the shoes of peace had materialized—along with the rest of my armor.

I immediately stopped and drew my sword. I scanned the horizon for the enemy, but there was none to be seen. It would be hard to see *anything* out here—much less a black shadow. I wasn't afraid, though; I'd practiced with my sword. I was prepared.

"Come on out, I know you're there," I called to the invisible being. "There's no use hiding."

I received no response.

"Come on," I said impatiently, tapping my shoe on the dusty dirt road. "I don't have all night. Let's get this over with."

Still nothing.

"If you're waiting for me to ignore you, and continue on, I'm not going to do it," I told it. "I know you'll just attack me as soon as my back is turned, and I'm not going to give you that opportunity."

Nothing.

This was strange. Usually by this point, the sombra would have acknowledged itself. Once it's been found out, a sombra typically finds no more reason to hide. Plus, I had found that sombras don't like to be branded a coward; most would rather engage in a fight and end up dead than to hide from the danger.

So why was this sombra hiding?

I was starting to feel a little uneasy—something was not right. Something about this bothered me. Despite the fact that I was wearing my armor, I didn't feel protected like I usually did. I felt vulnerable.

My eyes darted in every direction—looking for any sign of danger. *If only there was more light out here!* I thought to myself. But it was fast becoming darker with every passing second.

That's when I saw it: In the distance, about twelve feet off the ground, were two red lights suspended in midair. They were barely visible in the darkness, but I saw them. They glowed like fire, but I knew I wasn't looking at fire.

I was looking at eyes.

I had never seen such eyes. I had never seen so much hatred contained in one place before. They were blood-red, but not like Espíritu's fiery eyes. These burned with an entirely different kind of intensity. I felt suddenly that there was nothing left for me but to die.

Wait a minute, I corrected myself. *I'm a* warrior! *A warrior of the* King! *I don't have to be afraid!*

"I can see you!" I shouted at the eyes. "And I'm ready for you! I don't care *how* big you are—with the help of the King, I can bring you down! This day the King will deliver you up into my hands! I'm ready for anything you're prepared to throw at me, so *bring it on!*"

The next moment I was reconsidering my words as I saw the thing materialize. As darkness slowly formed around the eyes, a dark shape began to appear. It was a sombra, all right—but what a sombra! This sombra stood thirteen feet tall…its gigantic wings spreading out from its body causing it to appear twice as large as it really was.

My first instinct was to run, but my legs seemed frozen where they were. Besides, where could I run where this creature couldn't follow?

My thoughts were interrupted by a noise. I looked at the shadow; was the noise coming from the sombra? It sounded like deep breathing.

What was happening? I blinked a couple times; the shadow was changing shape. It no longer appeared as a thirteen-foot-tall man with wings but as…as a what? The lines were poorly defined—it was still changing. All I knew was that it was getting wider and taller; it was too dark out here to see clearly. I watched the eyes; the eyes remained steady and unchanging—always burning, always piercing.

I watched as the clawed hands grew to fifty times their size. I watched as the black wings spanned the distance from the house to the barn. I watched as the neck became elongated—stretching up into the sky—the head bent down, forming an arc. What was that long, black object that wriggled on the ground like a snake next to the massive body? It was a tail.

I was looking at a dragon.

The eyes suddenly moved—the dark head rising to its full height. The creature was staring down at me with absolute hatred. It was waiting to attack and destroy me, and I must subdue it.

But somehow the idea of subduing this creature seemed ludicrous.

I knew who this sombra was. I knew who it was that I was looking at; there was no doubt in my mind.

This was the leader of the sombras. This was Mentiroso.
"Father, help me," I breathed.
I would definitely need it this time.

CHAPTER 42

The Final Battle

The battle began almost immediately. The first fiery dart was thrown at me—not from his hand but from the dragon's mouth—in a long, steady stream. I'd had my shield of faith ready and so I was not burned. The blow had thrown me to the ground, and I stood back up.

"'Therefore put on the full armor of the King,'" I shouted up at the monster, "'so that when the day of evil comes, you may be able to stand your ground, and after you have done everything, to stand.'"

A moment later, I was no longer standing but lying on my back again. I got up.

"'Submit yourselves, then, to the King,'" I called to him. "'Resist Mentiroso, and he will flee from you.'"

The dragon apparently didn't like that verse either; this time the flame sent me rolling along the ground for several feet. When I'd stopped, I examined the damage: my armor was somehow remaining unscorched throughout all of this.

I stumbled to my feet. The dragon had already quickly advanced towards me and was preparing another fiery dart.

"'The Prince of peace will soon crush Mentiroso under your feet.'"

The dragon *really* didn't like this verse; the fire from his mouth seemed to burn with extra intensity this time.

I wasn't sure how much more of this I could take. The last blow had sent me rolling again and my stopping point had been the trunk of a tree. Were it not for my helmet of salvation, the impact would have very likely knocked me unconscious. As it was, I was just barely able to make out a black shape coming towards me.

"'Resist Mentiroso...'"

The steady stream of fire practically welded me into the trunk of the tree. My back was uncovered; I could feel the rough bark grazing its way through my shirt and into my flesh. I wasn't getting burned, but the sheer heat of the fire was making me hot and miserable. Sweat poured down my face and got in my eyes, but I couldn't wipe it away because the visor was in the way. And I dared not lift it.

I suddenly discovered another reason for why I felt so hot: I smelled smoke and realized that the tree behind me was on fire! I stood achingly to my feet and stumbled back away from the tree—dumbly staring at it. The enemy took advantage of my moment of distraction and caught me off guard with my shield down. I felt the fire this time as it ignited my shirt. I cried out in pain and dropped to the ground—rolling on my back as I had been taught to do. This was excruciatingly painful since my back was already rubbed raw from the bark of the tree. The fire was out now, but my back still felt like it was on fire.

The dragon didn't wait for me to get up. Another fiery blast was sent my way. Fortunately, I'd had the presence of mind to painfully lift my left arm—bringing the shield of faith over my body so that I was completely covered when the flame hit. My body was not touched, but I found myself driven a few inches into the ground afterward.

I somehow found the strength to climb my way out of my premature grave. I'd been fired at six times now, and I was feeling the effects of it. Thoughts of despair began to flood my mind, but I would not succumb to them. "'Stand your ground,'" I told myself. "I've got to *stand!*"

The devilish sombra didn't give me a chance; I felt another blast from the dragon's throat. However, I was amazed to find that—even though the blast was probably as powerful as before—I was not sent rolling this time; I merely fell backwards.

But I wasn't going to remain there. "'Stand your ground,'" I quoted once again, staggering to my feet.

I felt the impact of the next blast even less than before. I merely stumbled back a few steps. *I was still standing!*

"'Stand your ground,'" I quoted to Mentiroso.

What was this? Had the dragon just fired at me? If so, I hadn't felt it. I had heard the sound of the flame hitting my shield, but that was all. I hadn't felt a thing—not the slightest pressure against my shield.

My courage was renewed. "'No weapon formed against me shall prosper,'" I emphatically told the dragon.

The dragon decided to find out if that was true and fired again. He found out that it was true.

"'I can do all things through the Prince who strengthens me.'"

The dragon tried to fire at me, but the flame burned itself out before it ever reached me.

"'If the King is for us, who can be against us?'" I quoted, reaching for my sword.

Mentiroso answered by sending me another blow, but it was not a very forceful blow. The dragon was losing his power.

"'Finally, be strong in the King and in his mighty power,'" I said, drawing my sword. "'Put on the full armor of the King so that you can take your stand against the enemy's schemes.'"

My shield of faith served merely as a buffer now as I advanced towards the dragon.

"'For our struggle is not against flesh and blood,'" I reminded Mentiroso, "'but against the rulers, against the authorities, against the powers of this dark world and against the spiritual forces of evil in the heavenly realms.'"

I wondered for a moment why the dragon didn't try some other means of attack—like clawing or biting. Then it occurred to me: the dragon *had* no other means of attack. Clawing and biting hadn't worked for the other sombras; it wouldn't work for Mentiroso. Fuego was right: Mentiroso couldn't touch me.

"'Therefore,'" I shouted up at the creature, delivering the final blow, "'put on the full armor of the King, so that when the day of evil comes, you may be able to stand your ground, and after you have done everything, to stand.'" I was standing in the King's power now, and nothing could make me fall.

The proud sombra refused to back away. It was his own undoing.

The sword of Espíritu pierced the darkness. The giant creature screamed and suddenly everything went black as my vision was filled with one of Mentiroso's massive clawed hands. The next thing I knew I was lying face-down in the dirt about 30 yards from the dragon.

I watched from a distance as the creature struggled— writhing in pain. The red eyes looked at me with burning hatred as the dragon attempted in vain to send one final blast my way.

But it would never happen. The terrible head fell to the ground.

The battle was over. I could breathe freely now. The creature was dead.

Or so I thought. As if to get in one final word, the head

suddenly rose and came straight towards me—jaws open wide.

The head never reached me, for suddenly there was a bright light as a look of utter terror filled those blood-red eyes. What was he looking at? I closed my eyes and shielded them from the blinding light and the flying dust. All I could hear was high-pitched screaming and the sound of pounding hoofs.

Then it stopped. Slowly, I uncovered my face and dared to look. Through the settling cloud of dust, I could see that the dragon was gone. In his place was another figure— standing tall and strong and bright. It was in the shape of a giant horse with wings.

"Espíritu!" I cried, jumping to my feet. Somehow, all the pain and discomfort had disappeared along with my armor.

I threw my arms as best I could around this One whom I had come to know and love. "Espíritu, you're here!" I cried. "You *saved* me!"

I looked up into his fiery red eyes, still aflame. But these eyes did not burn with hatred—they burned with love. I trusted these eyes.

Now that Espíritu was here, I didn't have to think twice about what to do next. Seizing his long, white mane in my hands, I leapt onto his back.

"Let's go!" I shouted.

CHAPTER 43

Return to Paraíso

Paraíso was just like I remembered except…weren't the trees covered in leaves of gold before? This time they were covered in white, and the blossoms were falling like snow all around—despite the fact that there was no wind. And it seemed as though no matter how many fell, the trees remained just as white. *The seasons must have changed*, I thought. *Now it's springtime in Paraíso…or maybe in this* part *of Paraíso it's springtime.* As far as I could see in every direction, a forest of white and orchid lay around me—for the color of the trees' bark was an orchid, purplish color.

And I smelled a delicious smell. It smelled like food. I looked around to see where the smell was coming from. There in the distance—amid the white, falling blossoms—a long table had been set up and many wonderful things to eat were sitting on it: meats and cheeses and vegetables and breads and grapes. But what amazed me even more than the feast was the sight of those who feasted: seated around the table were at least two dozen big, strong guys with wings and swords—acting just as jovial as children. I had never before seen criados behaving this way. They were joking and talking (with their mouths full, at times) and laughing so hard that a few of them were literally getting carried away by their own wings and were finding themselves hovering above the table before they'd even realized what had happened. Their friends had to remind them and help them back down.

I thought I recognized one of them. "Sara!" Mensajero called to me from the air. (He was one of the ones who had gotten carried away.) "Sara, hello!"

I was a little embarrassed as some of his friends turned around and looked at me. As soon as he had been helped down, Mensajero sprinted over to me in a half run, half fly. "Sara, you've returned!" he said, coming to a halt directly in front of me and dropping to a knee. "How nice to see you here again!" I could tell he was suppressing a hug. Actually, I wouldn't have even minded too much.

I smiled and pointed towards the table. "Celebrating a birthday?" I joked sheepishly.

Mensajero's eyes lit up. "Actually," he exclaimed boisterously, grinning from ear to ear, "that is *exactly* what we are doing, little one! What brings you back to Paraíso so soon?"

"Well, Espíritu, of course!" I laughed.

He laughed along with me—a little surprised, I think, to see me joking and so full of joy. I was a little surprised myself.

"Actually," I responded, "there *is* a reason I'm here." I reached into my shorts pocket and pulled out the smaller version of the Book of Light. "Will you give this to Risa?" I asked him. "She's a citizen here. Tell her I'm one, too. Tell her thank you—that she's right: the Book of Light really *is* the greatest treasure in the world. Tell her that it saved my life…" I paused, choking back tears. "…and maybe the life of my Dad."

Mensajero could control himself no longer and gently

drew me close. "Do you know," he responded after several seconds. "It now occurs to me, Sara: there is a citizen of Paraíso here whom we call Risa. She gave me explicit instructions on what I was to do the next time I saw you." He reached into his long, draping white robe and pulled out a flower—placing it in my hand in exchange for the Book of Light. It was the most beautiful red rose I had ever seen. "I was to give this to you along with this message: 'Tell her to give this to her dad,' Risa told me. 'Tell her that he did not accept it from me at one time, but that now he has learned how to accept free gifts.' I know not what the message means, Sara, but she assured me that you would."

"Tell her that he did not accept it from me at one time..." It took a moment for the words to sink in. Then I suddenly recalled the story Dad had told me of how he and Mom had met. I remembered him telling me about how Mom had tried to offer him a rose, but that he didn't take it—although he wished that he had.

Then another thought occurred to me: Didn't Dad say that Mom had referred to the Book of Light as "the greatest treasure in the world"? Just like Risa...

Could Risa be...?

This time, the tears found their way out.

Mensajero, not understanding but feeling compassion for me just the same, reached up and gently wiped away my tears with his giant hand. "Some day," he spoke softly, "the King will wipe away every tear from your eyes."

I had felt that I could cry forever, but now the tears seemed to dry up and I found that I could speak. "Mensajero," I told him, "I have to go back to Earth now. I have to live there a little while longer before coming to live here. But before I do..." I looked down at the ground; I didn't want to be looking at Mensajero's sapphire eyes as I said it. "I was wondering if you could do me a favor."

"Anything, Sara," he responded. "You are the King's

daughter now; by serving you I serve the King."

"Could—could you make it so that I don't have the Power of Paraíso anymore?"

I dared to look up at him, expecting a look of confusion. But I think he understood.

"Very well, Sara," he responded. "But you do realize, I suppose, what it would mean? You would no longer have the ability to see things from Paraíso's point of view. You would no longer be able to see the criados...or the armor...or the light from the Book of Light..."

"...or the sombras," I finished for him.

He nodded. He understood.

"Then close your eyes, Sara," he told me.

I closed them. I felt his hand as it covered both of my eyes.

When I opened them again, I found myself standing on top of an upside-down old tin water bucket next to a wooden gate; Big Thunder was standing nearby, waiting for me to scratch his nose.

"Sara, it's getting dark out there," I heard Aunt Sarah call to me. "It's time for you to come inside now."

I looked around me. I was back—at least for now. Until Espíritu came back for me.

For a moment, I wondered whether Paraíso had been just a dream—a very sweet dream from which I was just now waking up. Then I looked down at the red rose in my hand. No, Paraíso was definitely *not* a dream.

I jumped down from the water bucket and started for the house. On the way, I looked up at the sky; the stars were just beginning to come out. On the horizon were purple and pink stair-step clouds.

I smiled. "I'm going to go back there some day," I said to myself.

I ran and joined Aunt Sarah waiting for me in the doorway and we walked into the house together.

* *

Dad and I left the next morning for home. But I knew I wasn't *really* going home. Home for me was Paraíso.

It could have been my imagination, but I thought I was beginning to see a familiar light shining in Dad's eyes. Who knows? Maybe they would begin to burn the way Espíritu's did. Sometimes I meet a stranger on the street with a mysterious light shining in their eyes, and I know at once of the great adventure they have had.

I no longer grieve for my mother—wishing she were still alive. I know beyond the shadow of a doubt that she lives now in a much better place.

I oftentimes find myself looking up at the sky in hopes that I might see a great white horse with wings coming to take me home. Once I thought I did, but it turned out only to be a faraway cloud. But I haven't stopped searching, because I know now that greater things await me in a world somewhere beyond the clouds. I do, after all, love watching the sky—and I *do* love white horses.

LaVergne, TN USA
18 September 2009
158334LV00003B/4/A